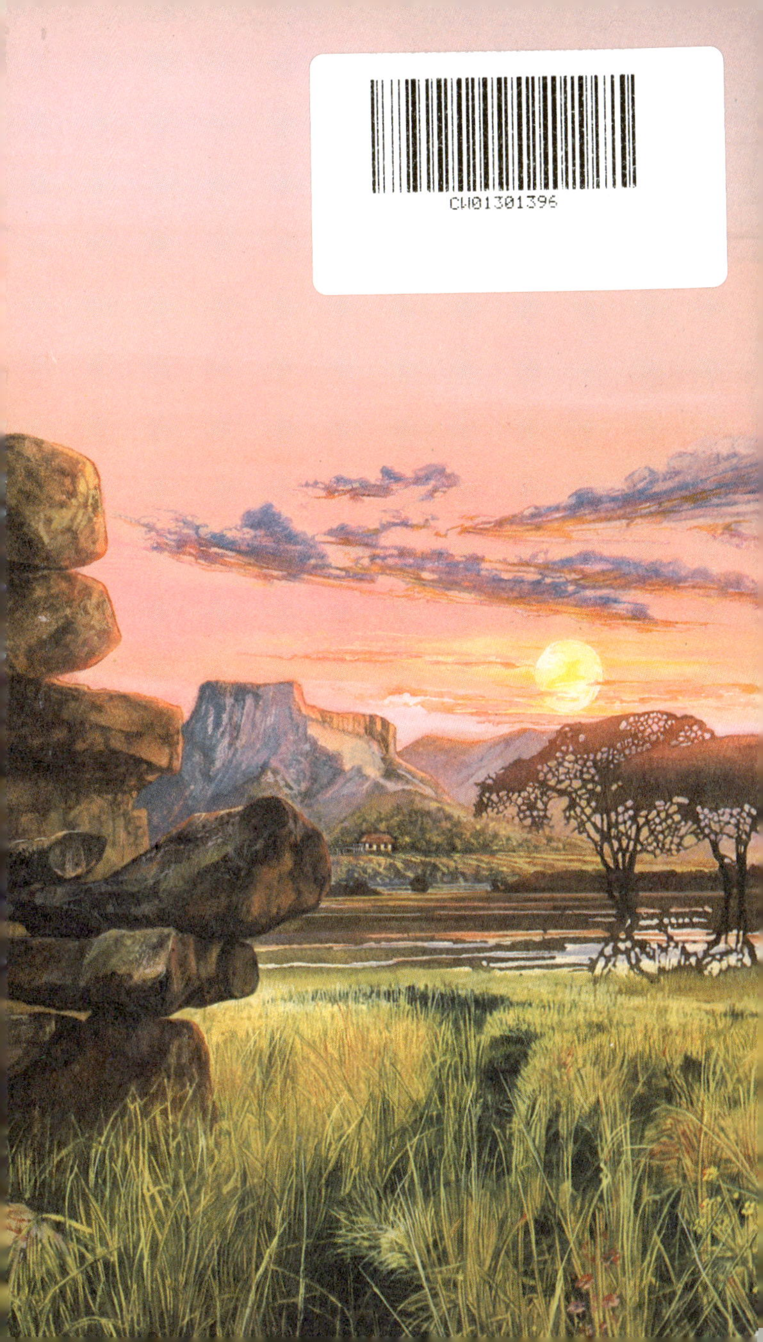

Daniel Carney, the son of a British diplomat, was born in Beirut in 1944. He grew up in the Far East and was educated in England. He travelled extensively throughout the world before settling in Zimbabwe in 1963. After a career as an estate agent he turned to full-time writing. He is the author of *Under a Raging Sky*, *The Wild Geese* and *The Square Circle* (filmed as *Wild Geese II*), all of which have been filmed or are in pre-production. His latest novel, *Macau*, is also available from Corgi Books.

Also by Daniel Carney

MACAU
UNDER A RAGING SKY
THE WILD GEESE
THE SQUARE CIRCLE

and published by Corgi Books

Daniel Carney

The Whispering Death

CORGI BOOKS

THE WHISPERING DEATH
A CORGI BOOK 0 552 11353 0

First published by The College Press (Pvt) Ltd., Salisbury, Rhodesia
First published in Great Britain by Pan Books Ltd.

PRINTING HISTORY
College Press edition published 1969
Pan Books edition published 1972
Corgi edition published 1980
Corgi edition re-issued 1985

Copyright © 1969 by Daniel Carney

Conditions of sale
1: This book is sold subject to the condition that it shall not, by way of trade *or otherwise*, be lent, re-sold, hired out or otherwise *circulated* without the publisher's prior consent in any form of binding or cover other than that in which it is published *and without a similar condition including this condition being imposed on the subsequent purchaser.*

2: This book is sold subject to the Standard Conditions of Sale of Net Books and may not be re-sold in the U.K. below the net price fixed by the publishers for the book.

Set in Intertype Baskerville

Corgi Books are published by Transworld Publishers Ltd., Century House, 61–63 Uxbridge Road, Ealing, London W5 5SA, in Australia by Transworld Publishers (Aust.) Pty. Ltd., 26 Harley Crescent, Condell Park, NSW 2200, and in New Zealand by Transworld Publishers (N.Z.) Ltd., Cnr. Moselle and Waipareira Avenues, Henderson, Auckland.

Printed and bound in Great Britain by
Cox & Wyman Ltd., Reading, Berks.

Dedicated with love to Leone

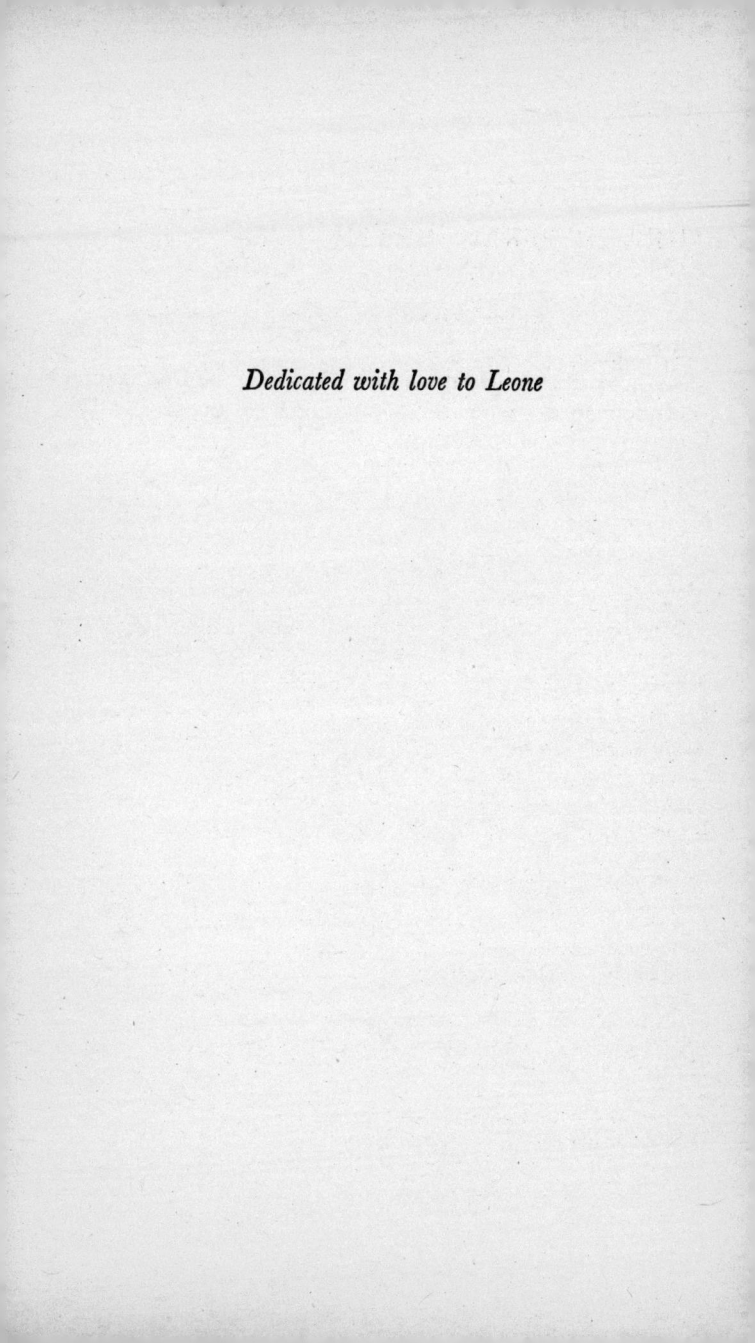

This book is set in Rhodesia some time after the Declaration of Independence when the population faces an ever increasing rise in acts of terrorism ...

CHAPTER ONE

THE prisoner spent his last night on earth in a small, bare cell on the second floor of the death block in Salisbury Gaol. He was young, about twenty-four, tall and hard, his face burnt dark-brown by the sun. His hair was also brown, with startling flashes of white on either temple, and he wore a faded prison uniform, open at the neck. He was sweating slightly and his shirt was damp in patches.

He sat quietly on his cot. His eyes were a deep, haunting blue and they wandered restlessly over the cell, from the grey stone floor up the bare, white-washed walls to the high white ceiling from which, protected by an iron grille, a naked light bulb burned.

A warder sat by the door. He was old, with a tired but kindly face. He had sat there many times before.

'Do you want to talk, play cards or something?' the warder asked. 'You know, I still think that you should have some kind of minister,' he appeared embarrassed, 'to sort of, well, help you on your way.'

The prisoner shook his head.

'Right you are then! But I'd go to sleep if I were you – it's better that way. You don't worry so much.'

From the depths of his uniform pocket the warder pulled out a battered paperback and started to read, his lips forming the words.

The prisoner moved over to the window. Grasping the bars in either hand he pressed his face between them and up against the window pane. For the first time in many months he could see over the tall, barbed-wire-capped prison walls to the free world beyond.

In the vlei beyond the walls the elephant grass swayed to

a light evening breeze and his ears caught the distant sound of the crickets. He stood in silence, and it seemed as though all the prison was silent with him.

The prisoner remained staring sightlessly out between the prison bars into the gathering darkness. He had killed twenty-three men over the space of four days – an act, as the prosecutor put it, of premeditated vengeance that could only be requited by the death sentence. Throughout his trial the prisoner had refused to say anything in his defence. And now the last hours of his life were ticking away.

Suddenly, as though he had made some great decision, he turned from the window and walked lightly across the room to where the warder was sitting. He touched the warder gently on the shoulder. The warder started. Impatiently the prisoner motioned him up and, as the warder rose, the prisoner pushed the chair into the centre of the room and placed it against the wall. He turned to the warder and motioned him to sit. The warder sat nervously clutching his book.

With his cot, bedclothes and anything else he could find, the prisoner fashioned himself a crude courtroom. The warder started to protest.

'Be quiet,' the prisoner whispered. 'You're the judge.'

The warder started up. 'Blimey,' he muttered softly to himself, 'the bugger's gone mad.'

He moved slowly towards the door, trying to face the prisoner at the same time. In two strides the prisoner reached him and gripped his arm. The warder jumped.

'It's all right, it's all right, I'm not going to hurt you,' the prisoner said gently. 'I just want to tell my side of the story before I die. Listen, will you? It's important to me.'

At first the warder was reluctant, but there was something in the prisoner's voice that reassured him and he allowed himself to be led back to his chair.

'All right, but put the furniture back then.'

The prisoner shook his head.

'No. I want this to be like a court. I'll tell you how it really happened. How I felt – how much she means to me. Then, at the end, you give me your verdict.'

The warder shrugged his shoulders. Then he bowed to the prisoner, who took up his position on a blanket which was to act as the accused's box.

'You may proceed,' he said solemnly.

'Thank you, my lord.'

The warder settled back into his chair. He was beginning to enjoy himself and the retelling of this story might earn him a few free beers. Anyway it would help the night to pass.

'My lord,' they bowed to one another. 'Gentlemen of the jury...'

The prisoner was standing directly in the path of the moon's rays as they filtered through the barred window, and glinted silvery off his head and shoulders, setting an eerie scene. His eyes grew wistful. Then he cleared his throat.

CHAPTER TWO

It started on the day that I left the Police Force. That was just five days before my wedding day, four months ago. And yet I can see it all so clearly now...

The rains were late and the little bush police station lay shimmering whitely in the heat of the morning sun. I had just handed in my kit and, followed by Sailor, my dog, was making my way across the little green square in front of the station when Peter came striding towards me.

He was an enormous man, a little older than myself, weighing about two hundred and forty pounds of solid bone and muscle. His face was startlingly ugly, with enormous ears that stood out at right-angles from his temples and a shock of sandy hair that covered his forehead. Women found him attractive. Perhaps it was because his ugly features radiated warmth and humour and sincerity that you instinctively liked him. He spoke and acted slowly but with a great singleness of purpose, and when he ran out of words he was apt to use his fists. We had joined the Police Force together, I a stranger from England and he from an isolated farm in the bush. I would have walked from here to China to lend him my last five pounds, and he would have done the same for me.

'Hey,' he said. 'I've been looking for you. The big mambo wants you.'

'What for?'

Peter shrugged his shoulders. 'How should I know? He just poked his head around the door and yelled "Hurndell". Perhaps he wants to say goodbye or something.'

I shook my head. 'Hardly. He's coming to the piss-up tonight.'

Peter grinned. 'Well then perhaps he wants to hear more about this White renegade you've been faffing about.'

'I suppose you find it funny, too.'

'Not me,' Peter said with uncharacteristic meekness, 'him.' He was grinning as he nodded towards the Member in Charge's window.

'You'll see,' I muttered as I strode past. 'You'll all bloody well see.'

'That's my boy,' Peter jeered after me. 'You tell him.'

I swung round, my fists clenched. 'Peter, so help me ...' But Peter was walking on down the path chuckling to himself.

I stopped outside a brown wooden door with a sign on it marked 'Member in Charge'. I paused for a moment, feeling faintly ridiculous in civilian clothes. Then I knocked firmly on the door.

A deep, slow voice said, 'Leave your dog outside.'

The office was small and bright, cluttered with files, typewriters, a safe in the corner with a fishing rod against it, and a huge oak desk which dominated the room. Behind it, with his feet resting on the top, sat the Member in Charge, a small portly man with a red face and greying hair who had married the Police Force some twenty years ago. He grunted, then, carefully removing his feet from the desk, motioned me to sit.

I gratefully removed his golf clubs and sat opposite him in an old wicker chair. He leaned back surveying me through a pair of sleepy grey eyes.

'That last patrol of yours.' He leaned over fumbling for it amongst the papers that cluttered the desk. 'Here.'

He thumbed through the pages until he reached a paragraph he had underlined in red. He motioned me closer.

'Here,' he pointed with the stem of his pipe, 'you say that the kraals in the area around the Devil's Playground are restless,' his voice grew ominously quiet, 'the people nervous, informers dried up.' He looked up at me. 'Just because the area is quiet for a change you immediately think they're scared.'

'Yes.'

'Why? Did the Chief tell you this?'

'No.'

'One of the headmen?'

'No.'

'Then who did?'

'No one, sir.'

'Then,' said the Member in Charge patiently, 'how do you know?'

'Well I . . . I felt it,' I waved my hand helplessly, 'sort of in the air.'

The Member in Charge leaned back in his chair thinking deeply. His grey eyes seemed flecked with black as they searched my face. Suddenly he jerked forward. Then he growled. 'There is this whisper that you heard,' he consulted the report, 'of some White renegade who claims that he's the spirit of Lobengula come to lead his people against the Europeans. Well, you've made a statement. Now where are the facts to back it up?'

'I made it perfectly clear in there, sir,' I pointed to the patrol report. 'There are no facts.'

The Member in Charge's fists came crashing down on the desk. Papers flew in all directions as he started up.

'Hurndell,' he shouted, 'I sent you on patrol to collect facts, not feel the bloody air.'

I started up, angry now. We faced each other across the desk. 'Sometimes,' I said slowly, 'sometimes when you walk through a kraal you can feel that there is something wrong. You can feel the nervousness of the people, but you can't put your finger on it.'

'And the renegade?' he prompted.

'A mad woman came to my camp one night and told me.' I sensed his disapproval.

'Yes, I know. But in the circumstances it made sense to me.'

Suddenly he leaned back in his chair. 'So you honestly believe all this,' he tapped the page with the stem of his pipe, 'mad woman and all.'

I nodded as I lowered myself slowly into my seat. For the first time in what had seemed a long while, a smile broke out across his face.

'Believe it or not, Terick, I have investigated your report.'

'Thank you, sir.' I was still angry. I didn't like being grilled. But he didn't seem to notice my interruption, for he carried on.

'I passed it on to Special Branch. They think I'm mad. I tried the Officer Commanding. He asked me when I'd last taken leave. I even tried the District Commissioner. He's ready to certify me.' The Member in Charge paused, frowning. 'Never did like that man. Everyone says I'm getting jittery.' He drew slowly on his pipe. 'Perhaps they are right.'

'Are you going to leave it at that?'

The Member in Charge shrugged. 'What more can I do? As it is, I had a very difficult interview with the OC. Can you imagine what it was like trying to convey your feelings to him?' The Member in Charge shook his head at the memory. 'No, he didn't take to it at all. But then why should he? We've no facts. As he pointed out, with so few Europeans in the area if one was involved Special Branch would know about it in a flash. As a matter of fact, in that,' he said slowly, 'I agree with him.'

I shook my head impatiently. 'Not a European, an albino.'

'An albino?' the Member in Charge considered the suggestion. Then he shook his head. 'They are an insipid bunch, poor bastards. I've never even heard of one getting into trouble with the law, let alone become a terrorist.'

'Well, sir, I have a theory.'

He smiled, for I was well known for my theories.

I leaned back in my chair and lit a cigarette, pausing to collect my thoughts.

'I know the country's quiet at the moment,' I conceded, 'and that the system of informers which we have been using to catch the terrorists is proving effective. Even in our area no stranger can enter a reserve without our being informed of his every movement. But on the other hand, the terrorists that were caught recently in the Zambezi Valley were much better trained. Remember the run they gave us? Now,' I leaned forward to press my point, 'suppose that over the last year an arms and food cache had been set up somewhere in the bush near here. A well-trained group of four or five men could cross the Zambezi without running into any of our patrols and then make their way across country, moving at night. They wouldn't have to enter a kraal for food until they reached their cache. From there they could equip and organize the young *tsotsis* without our knowledge. They never need lead an operation once they have proved themselves. All they have to do is appoint leaders, promise them anything and let them do the dirty work.'

'Get to the point,' the Member in Charge said.

'Well, if my theory is correct, the terrorists have to make a killing soon. They'll have to prove themselves before the *tsotsis* will pluck up enough courage to follow them.'

The Member in Charge nodded. 'And I suppose that you want me to call out the Police Reserve and put everyone on stand-by on the strength of your theory?'

'Yes.'

'Well now, listen to me. There are four Europeans and thirty Askari on this station. With them I have to cover thirty farms and a native reserve – altogether an area about the size

13

of Wales. Now,' he jabbed his pipe at me to ensure my complete attention, 'firstly, I haven't got enough men to keep up a stand-by for more than a few days. Secondly, if I cry "wolf" too many times they'll either get jittery or they'll lose their enthusiasm. Instead of forty Police Reservists turning up for training I'll get only five or six. The rest will make excuses. Lastly, and the most important point, is that there are only a few terrorists still operating in this country and they are way up to the north of us. The ones that have come down have been picked up by their own people and handed over to us, and there is nothing to indicate any sudden change of heart. If there were terrorists in our area we would know about it,' the Member in Charge said finally.

'But if a man were to go into the reserve and claimed that he was Lobengula's spirit,' I answered doggedly, 'if he could perform a few tricks, hold a few impressive ceremonies, he might be able to sway them or at least terrify them so much that they wouldn't hand him over.'

The Member in Charge smiled. 'Why Lobengula?'

'Remember that old folk-tale that they tell around here? Remember they say that he had a white soul and that's why he was such a great chief. You see, it all fits in.'

The Member in Charge laughed. 'It's a plausible story but I'm not convinced. Still, I'll send a few Askari into the reserve in plain clothes to ferret around.'

He stood up, signifying that the interview was over. 'Well, Terick,' he held out his hand, 'it's not your worry now, but don't mention this to anyone. You know how rumours spread. Even if you do say it's only a theory, by the time it's fourth-hand it's Gospel truth and the country's swarming with terrorists.'

'All right sir, but I still reckon it's more than a theory.'

The Member in Charge sighed.

'Is it all right if I leave the station,' I asked, by the door.

'You don't have to account to me any more.' Suddenly the Member in Charge grinned. 'Now get out of my office you bloody civilian, before I have to do any more reports in triplicate.' He shook his head. 'You know I always said you'd make a better farmer than a policeman. Good luck.'

Sailor was waiting for me under the shade of a tree by the stables and with him waited Katchemu, an old Matabele Askari who had adopted me on my arrival at the station some two years ago. He rose as I approached, a giant of a man with long sinewy arms that seemed to reach down to his knees, his hair greying and tightly crinkled, and his smile a little short of teeth.

'Mambo,' he said as he ambled over. 'We going to the Madam's now?'

'Yes, you handed in your kit?'

'Ja, Mambo.' A grin wrinkled his black, parchment-like face. 'I'm your boss boy from today.'

I am, partly by nature and partly from circumstance, a lonely man. I spent my childhood in English boarding schools or holiday homes, my parents nearly always being abroad. My father was a distant, awe-inspiring figure whose photograph, in plumed hat, full dress and sword, I proudly showed my friends. My mother was an equally distant but warmer figure, who poured out her love to me in weekly letters and presents that arrived unexpectedly.

When I was thirteen my mother died of cancer and the letters stopped. My father remained aloof and suddenly I found myself alone. I became conscious of a desperate need to be loved. At first I searched for it in the faces of the strangers that I met. I was vulnerable and, as the years passed, I grew up quickly. My pride forbade me to call on anyone. Instead, I turned inward and found the security that I needed within myself. Gradually I found that, far from needing people, I preferred to be alone.

On leaving school I received a generous allowance and went to London. The shallow, cynical mantle of a young man about town fitted easily on my shoulders. I went the usual rounds of parties and tried every vice that I could think of, and yet nobody could actually involve me. It was as though I were on the outside, watching.

One morning I awoke in a strange flat and watched a

strange girl dress for work. My mouth was furred with the stale taste of beer and cigarettes. I was bored and I decided to move on. That afternoon I went to Rhodesia House and joined the British South Africa Police.

Life on a small station suited me. The nearest tarred road was a hundred and ten miles away. If I needed companionship there was Peter or the mess. And when I needed to be alone there was always long patrols in the bush.

Then I met Sally. She attracted me immediately and in defence I avoided her. Her background was similar to mine except that she had been brought up by her grandfather. Apart from that we were totally opposite. She was as naïve as I was cynical, as warm as I was cold.

Later she told me that, after about the third time we met, she decided she was going to marry me. But I was very difficult to get to know. Every time she reached out I would retreat into my shell. And yet I enjoyed being with her.

Gently, patiently, she kept prodding at my defences until one day, more in fear than in anger, I lashed out at her. 'Leave me alone!' Couldn't she be satisfied with my company? Did she have to possess my soul as well? I saw the hurt cross her face. I stormed out and took myself off to the bush for a couple of weeks.

Out there I suddenly found that I cared that I had hurt her. I stayed away for as long as I could, then sheepishly I came back and the roles were reversed. I grudgingly began to court her.

Little by little I began to give of myself, until one day, half-angry because I felt naked and defenceless, and half-frightened in case she refused, I asked her to marry me. I remember I stood before her with my hands gripping her arms so tightly that my fingers left weals on her flesh. She accepted quietly without showing any surprise and I wondered how someone so small could exert so much power over me.

From then on I offered her all the love and warmth and trust stored up in me that I never knew I possessed.

I parked beneath a sheer rock-face and started up the winding stone stairway that led to the farmhouse, perched like a fortress on the top. I was about halfway when I heard the patter of feet racing down the steps towards me and Sally appeared from round the corner. She was the same height as my shoulder with a slender yet full figure and long, chestnut hair that spilled carelessly down her back. Her mouth was wide and sensuous and her lips curved upwards with the creases of a smile in the corners. But it was her eyes that made her beautiful. They were wide and dark and they seemed to change colour with the light, so expressive that they could almost talk.

In one fluid movement she handed me the lunch basket, threw her arms around my neck and kissed me. I hugged her until she bit my ear to make me let her down. For a moment we stood looking at each other. Then her hand reached up, gently brushing across my face and lifted the hair off my forehead.

Katchemu was waiting for us as we reached the bottom of the stairway.

'Darling,' Sally whispered suddenly, 'don't let Katchemu come.'

'Madam,' Katchemu nodded gravely as Sally approached him.

'How are you, Katchemu? How are your children?'

'Madam, they are well.' His face dropped. 'They are all eating too much. Unless I get them married soon I'll be a poor man.'

Sally laughed. 'Well, then, how's your second daughter – the one who's just got married?'

'Ah, that one,' Katchemu scowled. 'There's been plenty of trouble over the payment of her lobola. Every month now her husband has said that his crops have failed or that his cattle are sick and he cannot afford to pay her marriage price. It cost me too much to feed that one,' he grumbled.

'Perhaps the husband is telling the truth about his crops,' Sally said, trying to pacify him.

'No,' Katchemu answered indignantly. 'He is trying to

cheat me.' Suddenly he grinned and his bloodshot eyes rolled.

'Don't worry, Madam,' he reassured her cheerfully, 'if he doesn't pay soon I'll break his skull in, sure.' He made a chopping motion with his hand. 'Then I'll find her another husband.'

'If you do that,' Sally said and her eyes twinkled, 'she might find it difficult to find another husband.'

'Katchemu,' I cut in before he could reply, 'we're riding over the farm. Make your way to the compound and make sure that the boys are settled in. We'll start work tomorrow morning.'

'Am I not going with you?'

'No, you're the boss boy now,' I reminded him.

He turned and wandered off. 'I'll see you back here at sundown,' I shouted after him. He half-raised his hand to show that he had heard.

'Why,' Sally asked, staring after him, 'of all the people you could have chosen from, did you have to make that bloodthirsty old savage your boss boy?'

'The men respect him,' I answered briefly.

Katchemu's record of service used to make the Member in Charge wince. He had spent more time in the cells or undergoing various forms of punishment than any other Askari on the station. Most of the charges were minor, relating to discipline, for Katchemu regarded no man as his superior regardless of rank or colour. But his main vice was drink. A heavy bout usually ended in a fight and then a brief sobering-up period in the cells. His opponent usually spent his recovery period in the local clinic.

When I first arrived at the station a report came in that an outlying kraal was brewing skokian. The police usually reacted sharply to this because a particularly potent brew could drive a man blind, or mad. I was sent to stop it and Katchemu was detailed to accompany me.

We arrived at the outskirts of the kraal after nightfall and I was informed that the inhabitants had been drunk for three days as a mark of respect for an elder who had died recently.

The secret is to make straight for the 44-gallon drums containing the skokian and tip them up before the startled crowd can move. Then you turn and face them, hoping that the respect they bore your predecessor, and their fear of retaliation if they touch a policeman, will prevent them from tearing you apart. The Rhodesian Police don't carry guns and even if you did have one it wouldn't be much use against five hundred angry Africans. There is a further secret, however, which I learned later, and that is to make them laugh. An African laughs easily and once you have managed this the tension is broken and the guilty brewers allow themselves to be arrested quite happily.

I managed to tip up the drums all right. But, when I turned to face them, all I could see was a seething crowd of drunken Africans, their faces contorted with rage. The average drum of skokian, with its odd collection of rats and snakes floating around in it to enhance the flavour, is worth up to ten pounds to the brewer. Besides I had spoiled a good party.

There was an icy silence and the tension rose unbearably. I stood petrified, staring back, but for the life of me I couldn't think of anything to say. Suddenly one of them, a stranger in the area, elbowed his way through the crowd. He was a little smaller than I, but built like a weight-lifter. He gave an ear-splitting yell and lunged at me. The crowd moved forward with him, but a low, almost animal-like growl, stopped them dead.

Katchemu reached into the fire and pulled out a flaming log half as tall as himself and as thick as his thigh. He brandished it warningly.

Then the stranger was on me. His first punch knocked me flat on my back and my cap rolled off. I rolled clear of the kick that he launched at my ribs and scrambled to my feet. I was not as concerned about being hurt as about my loss of dignity. A few more punches and well-placed kicks soon cured me of that and I began to fight in earnest. But it was an unequal battle from the start. No matter how hard I hit him the man was so drunk that I couldn't hurt him, even though my knuckles cut his face to ribbons. The skokian seemed to lend him more and more strength.

At last, when I could hardly hold my hands up any more, he threw himself at me, his fingers closing around my throat, and I landed on my back in the fire with him on top of me.

I could hardly see because the blood was clotted in my eyes but I smelt my flesh burning. The pain gave me the last reserve of strength to throw him off. I don't remember much of the fight after that, but I ended up by beating his head against a rock until he lost consciousness.

I managed to rise to my feet, found my cap and put it firmly on my head. Then I staggered out of the kraal and into the bush where I collapsed.

Katchemu found me and carried me down to a spring where he cleaned me up, chuckling to himself.

'You weren't much help,' I lisped angrily between my broken lips.

He just grinned and looked me up and down as if to say 'you'll do'.

'It was a good fight,' he commented eventually. 'Next time, even if you go back alone, there will be no more trouble with you.'

After that we just seemed to drift together. If I were going on a patrol it seemed natural that he would come too. We were both rather silent men and rarely talked to each other unless we had something important to say.

When I decided to leave the police Katchemu handed in his ticket and announced that he was coming with me.

'Hey!' It was Sally. She had been talking and I had not replied. She tossed her head and her eyes flashed. It was a sign of trouble that I'd come to know well. Sally was not the sort of girl to be taken for granted. I reached out and took her hand. Then I grinned at her. 'Stop wittering at me, woman,' I said cheerfully.

Old Joseph, the head groom, was hanging onto the reins of my horse, a seventeen-hand hunter with bunches of muscle that rippled beneath his glossy brown coat.

'Be careful, Mambo,' he warned, his leathery face peering anxiously up into mine. 'With a horse like this you can race the wind.'

As soon as my seat touched the saddle, the grooms stood clear and we were off, the sparks flying as the horse's hooves struck the cobbles and the wind shaking out his mane. I felt a surge of power gather in his haunches as we cleared the low brick wall surrounding the stables and galloped across the paddock by the edge of the dam, scattering herds of steers in our path. For a quarter of a mile I let him run, feeling the warm wind in my face and the earth pounding beneath his hooves. Then I began to slow down.

Sally caught up within a minute. Her hair had come free from her scarf and was flying out behind her. She was almost round an outcrop of rocks before I spurred my horse forward. Suddenly he reared and I lost my balance. As I fell, I caught the flash of a snake whipping over the dirt. I slid heavily into the dust and lay there, winded.

When I sat up the snake had gone. My horse had moved off and was pulling up a patch of grass that grew in the shade of a nearby rock. There was no sign of Sally.

I walked cautiously up to the horse, gripped the reins and hauled myself onto his back. I urged him into a canter and we followed the path winding in and out of the rocks and stunted mopani trees that littered the way. We moved deeper into the bush but still there was no sign of her.

After about a mile I reined my horse in. I stood in the stirrups and, cupping my hands, I called her name. My voice echoed, muffled against the rocks.

I called again louder. Then I dismounted and checked the hoof-prints in the sand. There were several sets of old prints leading in both directions but mine were the only fresh ones.

I couldn't have passed her. My mind retraced the route. There was only this path, no others leading off. My eyes searched around. The path which we were following was a short-cut, probably an old game trail, and it wound through a vast expanse of tangled waste ground that divided her grandfather's farm from mine. People called it the Devil's

Playground, and it was aptly named for I had never seen a bleaker stretch of land.

By some freak of nature the whole area was littered with gigantic granite boulders, some fifty feet high, with as many as three or four precariously balanced upon one another like castles in the air.

Every time I passed this way the landscape always moved me, somehow awed me, by its vastness and its silence. Scrub-lined kopjes and boulders standing so proud and desolate that they would never bear the scars of man. High above me hundreds of tons of solid rock balanced eternally on surfaces a few inches across, and scattered here and there grew fever trees, parched by the drought, their branches forming grotesque silhouettes against the shimmering skyline. And the wind moaned softly through the cavities in the rocks high overhead.

Occasionally the Africans would pass this way by day, in groups. At night they gave it a wide berth, for they claimed this whole area was haunted, each boulder representing the ghost of some long-forgotten war chief, and the moaning wind was their war song.

I felt the hair on the nape of my neck begin to prickle.

'Sally,' I called and in the eerie absence of any other living thing my voice was hushed.

I moved forward, searching for tracks. At last I found some. Sally's horse had galloped off the path a little, then back on. I saw the tracks veer off into the scrub and peter out. I followed.

At first the going was easy, far easier than I had thought. The ground had been stamped flat and the scrub grew small and sparse as though we were following some old path.

After a few hundred yards I stopped. I had entered a small clearing. Around me towered a solid, almost circular wall of rock. The elephant grass grew two feet taller than my head.

I shouted again.

'Sally!'

Suddenly, ahead I saw the tall grass sway and rustle and Sally's mare cantered into the clearing. I dismounted and caught the mare, running my hands over her for any signs of injury but there was not even a graze.

I stood holding the reins, my mind racing. There wasn't much that could have happened to Sally – she was an expert horsewoman. My thoughts kept coming back to terrorists. But in daylight . . . it was impossible.

I tethered the horses and walked slowly through the high grass. I paused for a second to pick up a heavy stick. I swung it a few times to test it weight. The club made a whirring sound above my head.

I walked, my arms outstretched to ward off the grass which opened before me and closed behind me leaving no trace of my passing. I went on blindly until I stumbled and fell, half-kneeling, onto the ground. When I looked up Sally was sitting on a rock watching me.

'Hello,' she said.

'Bloody fool. Where have you been?'

She smiled. 'I knew you'd find me. I wanted to show you something.'

'It had better be good.' I was angry.

'It is.' She reached for my hand and we walked through the grass until we reached the sheer rock-face. She pulled some grass away and pointed.

'Look.' In front of us was a carefully-concealed entrance to a small tunnel. 'It goes through the rock,' she said. 'You go ahead, and watch out for snakes.'

I hoisted myself up into the tunnel and wriggled forward on my belly. After about twelve feet I came out into the sunlight. Sally followed.

The ground was laid out in a circle, like an arena, with a thirty-foot wall of solid rock and boulders rising vertically all round. In the centre, smoothed by the wind and the rain, was a single rock shaped like a crude altar. The grass around it had been stamped flat.

I turned to her. 'How did you find it?' The walls amplified my voice and echoed it back.

'Disarki showed it to me. We used to play here when I was small. This is supposed to be the most haunted place of all.

The witch-doctors used it for their ceremonies. No one ever goes here now.'

'No,' I said and walked around. There was nothing on the altar but, when I kicked the soft dust around it, I found a pile of ashes.

'Is there another entrance?' I asked Sally.

She shook her head. 'The tunnel is the only one.'

Again I felt prickles down the back of my neck.

'Could be someone's still holding ceremonies here,' I said.

CHAPTER THREE

It was late afternoon when we left the Devil's Playground and cantered across an open stretch of ground heading for the farm I had just bought.

The ground before us sloped gently down to a small dam. On the other side we could see our cottage, built on the slopes of a tall kopje that rose in the distance.

All my savings – which weren't particularly impressive – had gone into buying the land. We could run five hundred head of Sally's grandfather's cattle on it, and every season I could pay him back some of the depressingly large loan which we had needed to get started, and buy some more.

We stopped by the dam and let the horses cool down and drink. Then we walked slowly up the slope.

We had built the cottage ourselves with earth taken from ant-hills, and the roof was thatched with grass. Sally had started a small flower garden in the front and was trying to grow vines up the walls.

I opened the front door and we walked into the sitting-room. At one end there was a large warm fireplace with a cast-iron gate which we had salvaged. The furniture, under white covers, was sparse. We couldn't afford much, but it was well laid out and the room had a bright, airy look.

Sally tugged at my hand and we walked through the rooms, peering into the cupboards and trying out the doors as though we were visiting the cottage for the first time. Our bedroom overlooked the dam and from its windows we could watch the sunrise in the mornings. All we had was a large double bed, a wardrobe and a dressing-table for Sally. Like the rest of the house it looked very bare, and yet, because it was mine, I loved every bit of it.

Next door I had already started the foundations of a nursery. I had built it far too large and Sally used to tease me about it. But I just used to look her up and down, and smile.

As we moved back into the sitting-room we found Sailor waiting for us, his paws dripping with water from the dam.

'Oh, no,' Sally groaned, looking at the floor where a row of muddy brown puddles led from the door.

'Tickey can clean it up when he comes tomorrow.'

'No.' Sally shook her head obstinately. 'I'll do it now. It won't take a second. Could you get some water? There'll be none in the taps now.'

I walked into the sunlight and drew some water from the well. When I returned Sally was waiting for me with a cloth in her hands.

'Darling, remind me, will you – I've left my ring on the mantelpiece.'

When she had finished I threw the water out and we started up the kopje.

I sat quietly on a large stone. To the east I could see way beyond the dam to the start of the balancing rocks in the Devil's Playground. For the rest, as far as the eye could see there was nothing. Nothing but miles and miles of rolling land stretching out into the horizon.

I felt many emotions well within me. For the first time in my life I felt as if I really belonged. And it was so much better because I had made it myself. It was as though the last dam deep inside me had broken and hundreds of dreams came tumbling out. One day, I told myself, I'm going to make that land down there come alive. It's going to teem with my cattle, and my children will play by that dam I built. Above all, there was no longer any need to be lonely.

'What are you thinking about?' Sally asked gently. I tried to tell her but the words still lay too deep for me to find them. I reached out and squeezed her hand.

'I'm glad I love you,' I said simply.

I got to my feet. 'Come on,' I said gruffly. 'It's time we were getting back.'

CHAPTER FOUR

ALL over the country now herds of wild game would be moving down to the water-holes to drink, and in the kraals the cooking fires would be lit. It was the cool of the evening – a time when a man could be alone with his thoughts.

I sat on the stoep of the old man's house watching the sun go down. There was a certain stillness in the air, a poignant emptiness before me. I watched the dying rays from the huge African sun dancing across the swaying elephant grass; in the distance were the Duvumbera mountains rising out of the veld. Duvumbera, I thought, even the name is beautiful.

I closed my eyes and listened to the night falling across the veld. In the distance I could hear the shouts of the herd boys as they moved the cattle into the paddocks, and the song of the crickets in the jacaranda trees. Down by the dam a bull-frog called for his mate. One day ... one day, I said to myself, my ranch will be like this.

The creak of a rocking-chair turned my head and I saw Sally's grandfather pouring out our sundowners. I watched him. He was an Afrikaner of about seventy, yet from the waist up he moved with the grace of a boy. His hair was white, his face tanned deep brown by the sun, his eyes a cool grey that seemed to see straight through you and way beyond. He was long and lean and hard. Yet a smile played in the corners of his mouth.

He handed me my drink and the first words of the evening were spoken.

'Man, but it's a strange world.'

I looked up and found him staring at me.

'Seventy years ago my father fought your grandfather for this land, or the land down south. Now their sons are liable to end up fighting side by side for the same bloody land. Doesn't make sense, does it?'

I shook my head.

'How do you feel about being a rebel?' he asked.

I took a deep draught of beer and it iced down my throat. I had often thought of this but it was difficult to put these thoughts into words, especially if you didn't understand them yourself.

I looked up at him and said, 'I suppose I don't really think of myself as a rebel or as a traitor or anything like that. I feel more like a son who's just disobeyed his father. I feel as though it's a family matter. I'm British and I'm proud of it, and if Britain were to go to war with any country other than Rhodesia I'd go and fight for her, so I don't see how I could be called a traitor. It's as though a son grows up and calls himself a man and he goes his own way; from that time on he may still love and respect his father but he makes his own decisions. When something like this crops up he must go to his father and say, "You brought me up, I have your standard of values. I'm doing something I believe in – something I believe to be right. Please try to understand." '

'And what happens?' the old man asked.

'Well, it seems to me that your father is so offended with your having disobeyed him in the first place that he doesn't try to understand what you're doing, or why you're doing it. He fights you every inch of the way, then the respect and love dies and only bitterness is left,' I said sadly.

'A man must do what he thinks is best and stick by it,' said the old man softly, and we both fell silent.

'How about you?' I asked eventually. 'How do you feel about UDI and sanctions?'

He rocked a bit harder and his brows knotted from thought. Then he began to speak slowly, choosing his words.

'Man, you must know. My family was of old Afrikaans stock until my son married Sally's mother, who was English. I never really had much schooling. I rather learnt life and the bush. There was no call to learn all these new-fangled things when I was young. Besides, we were always on the move trying to get away from you rooineks. Every time we moved north you'd follow us and build a town or something, and my father loved wide open spaces so we'd move again.

'My father taught us how to hunt and run a ranch; my mother taught us our schooling mostly from the Bible. I knew it backwards by the time I was fourteen. No,' he nodded slowly to himself, 'I didn't have much schooling with books and I'm not much good with words, but I can run a ranch as well as most men and that's all I need. Life was clearer in my day and you didn't argue with people by using long words and bits of history to prove your point. Nowadays I read the paper, when I can get it, trying to understand what they are saying until my eyes hurt. They keep contradicting themselves until my head spins and I get into such a temper that I'm liable to go out and fight the whole lot of them.'

He leaned forward, his fingers jabbing at me. 'Man, how can they understand how a man feels about his land; how he feels when he rides to the top of a kopje and looks for miles across his herds, his lands, a place he built from nothing with his own hands? See over there. My wife lies buried on the banks of that dam under that tree. My sons died fighting for England.' For a moment he looked sad then a fire lit in his eyes.

'Man,' he exploded, 'I'm telling you. How can a man from another country who buys his house from another man and then owns an acre of land – but who never had to fight for it, or make the bricks, or hew the wood to build it – understand me or how I feel? You ask me if I'll fight. Man, I've fought floods, I've fought droughts, I've fought sickness and disease, and you ask me if I'll fight! Here on this farm are fifty years of my life and here I'll die. If it comes from a bullet or old age, it doesn't make any difference. Nothing will make me move.'

I saw him getting more and more angry at the thought, so I asked him how he came to the country. It was a story that he loved to tell. His face brightened and his eyes grew wistful from the memory. Sally came in and put her arms fondly around her grandfather's shoulders.

'Drink up you two,' she said. 'Dinner's ready.'

Using his cane the old man struggled to his feet, shrugging off any attempts to help him, and limped towards the door. There he turned to me and smiled.

'Come,' he said, 'I'll tell you over dinner.'

We sat in his huge dining-room, lit by a wood fire and softly-hissing tilley lamps suspended from the ceiling. Over the fireplace hung a picture of his wife. She was beautiful and she seemed to move in every room as though her perfume still lingered in the air after all those years. The house had been built on and around a huge rock; in fact, you had to walk around it in the living-room. I asked him about it and, with a slow smile, he told me from a distance he had chosen this kopje as the site of his house.

'Man,' he said, 'then I got up here and found this rock in the way ... Now I couldn't move it, and here I was going to build my house. So I built over it. After all, I hadn't come all this way to be beaten by a bloody rock.'

The dinner was excellent and during it the old man told of how, many years ago, he had heard of this new country to the north of the Limpopo River where a man could carve himself out a place to call his own; where he could have as much land as a man could ride around in a day, if he had the guts to go and get it. He remembered way back to the day that he crossed the Limpopo with Dizarki, a horse, a rifle and fifteen shillings in his pocket. He was only sixteen years old, but, as he put it, he carried a dream in his heart.

He told of how he hunted elephant to make money, and with that he founded his dream, this ranch. He told of the good years and the bad ones; of the leopard that crippled him; of the deaths of his friends, his wife and children. I sat spellbound.

Later we moved into the living-room and sat before the fire. I swirled my brandy round in my glass, feeling its warmth within me, and watching the liquid sparkle in the firelight, while he cleaned one of his rifles. He was too lame to hunt any more but every night he sat and lovingly cleaned his rifles. I suppose he felt them part of his youth and he cherished the memories they gave him.

Sally, who had been surpervising the clearing away of the dishes, joined us and we sat silently hand in hand.

'Terick,' the old man said, 'I suppose that I'm considered by the district to be a pretty fierce old man?'

I nodded, 'You are.'

'And I suppose,' he continued gruffly, 'that when you first came courting Sally I gave you a pretty rough time?'

I grinned at him. 'You did. You used to point your rifles at me when you were cleaning them, remember?'

He smiled. 'They weren't loaded.'

I laughed softly. 'You know, I often wondered.'

'I had to be sure of you,' the old man said. 'You see I'm getting old now. I'm tired and I'm getting ready to die. My wife and sons – they're all dead.' He looked up and read our faces. 'No,' he said angrily, 'don't feel sorry for me. I'm not afraid of dying. Man, I've lived more in my life than any other ten men. It's just,' he continued more gently, 'it's just that, as I said. I'm tired. I'm a Christian and I haven't seen my wife in twenty years. I've got a lot to tell her when I get up there. She's a saint, you know,' he added gravely.

When his wife died, the old man in his grief personally canonized her, and the dominee of that time went in fear of being shot if he raised any objection.

'Besides I miss her,' he said softly. 'I've missed her for twenty years.'

Suddenly the old man shook his head impatiently.

'What I'm trying to tell you, Terick, is that all I've got left here is the farm and Sally.' He paused, looking deeply into the fire, and then continued slowly. 'When my sons were born I had dreams of leaving this ranch to them and their children and their children's children; of founding a small dynasty so that when I died I'd leave some small mark upon this earth, even if it were only a few acres of land and an ever-increasing family who bore my name.'

He smiled, 'I suppose that every man in some way would like to leave his mark upon this world, in the faces of his children, or in a painting, or in a ranch like this one out in the wilderness. No man just wants to crumble into dust and to be remembered only by his gravestone.'

Sally was biting her lip, fighting back her tears.

'Terick,' he growled, but a smile played in the corners of his mouth. 'Just you see that I'm proud of you.'

It was getting late and the fire had died to a glow. We sat silently drinking our coffee. There was nothing more to be said. The room was warm and we felt at ease. Then the grandfather clock by the door began to strike, its mellow chimes ringing out across the room. On the ninth and last stroke Dizarki entered the room. He was as tall as Sally's grandfather and nearly as old, with a long, lean, hawk-like face and dark piercing eyes. He crossed the room with a grace that betrayed great strength and his bearing was proud. Somewhere in his ancestry, I thought, there must have been a chief.

'My Mambo,' he reported to the old man, 'the cattle are safe, the compound is quiet and the farm is well for tonight.' They looked at each other with a liking and respect that had matured over fifty years.

'All right, Dizarki,' the old man nodded, but Dizarki did not move.

'My Mambo,' he said gently, 'it's time for you to go to bed now.'

'God damn it,' the old man growled, 'who do you think you are? My keeper or something?'

Dizarki took the wheelchair from the corner and placed it beside the old man.

'Well, answer me,' the old man roared.

Dizarki remained unmoved. 'My Mambo,' he said, and I never thought that his lean, hawk-like face could look so gentle, 'it is late and tomorrow is another day.'

Katchemu and Sailor were waiting for me as I climbed into the car. Then Sally came running down the steps.

'Darling, darling,' she sounded worried and I started up the steps to meet her.

'Oh darling,' she said breathlessly, 'I've left my ring behind ... at the cottage.' She pulled my hand. 'Let's go and get it.'

'Not a chance,' I said, 'that's two hours' ride away.'

'We can go by car the long way.'

I shook my head. 'We'll go and get it tomorrow morning first thing. Now I've got to go. I'm late already and Peter's going to murder me.'

'All right,' she nodded. Then her face brightened. 'Look darling, there's a full moon and it's a beautiful night for a ride. Couldn't I go alone?'

'No,' I growled. 'I'll not have you ride through those rocks at night.'

I kissed her and for a few seconds I stood looking at her in the moonlight, watching the rays dance in her eyes and on her hair.

'I love you,' I said softly. 'You're very, very, beautiful, especially in the moonlight.'

She waited until I reached the bottom of the steps. Then she waved goodbye and stood silently watching the car until it was out of sight.

I drove slowly across the old man's lands until I reached his boundary. There I stopped while Katchemu unlatched the five-bar gate. As he swung it open I glanced up, for there above the gate I could see a sign swinging in the night wind. I could see clearly in the moonlight an inscription painstakingly carved on it by hand. It read 'Johannes' Dream'.

CHAPTER FIVE

THE prisoner turned away from the little barred window. The moon was high overhead and the cell lay in dark shadow.

'Am I boring you?'

'No. No. Go on, go on,' the old warder said impatiently.

'I had to start at the beginning,' the prisoner said softly, 'so that you'd understand.'

'Do you want a glass of water or something?' the warder asked.

'No.' The prisoner turned his back to the window and placing his arms on the ledge he rested his chin upon them, staring out over the prison walls.

CHAPTER SIX

I STOPPED by a small compound a quarter of a mile from the Police camp where Katchemu was giving his own farewell party.

He climbed stiffly out of the car, surveying the compound with a practised eye. Several forty-four-gallon drums of seven-day brewed kaffir beer, foaming a thick muddy brown at the top, were scattered at convenient places around a circle of white sand. In the centre was a fire, and seated round it were some seventy or so people, waiting patiently for Katchemu to arrive. In the distance I heard a lone drummer warming up.

'Mambo,' Katchemu turned to me proudly, a gleam of anticipation lighting his eyes, 'this is going to be a big, big beer drink.'

African Sergeant Major Josiah joined us. He was a big good-natured man with a large stomach and a serious, conscientious nature. Though they had both joined the Police Force at the same time their differences in character had made him the Station Sergeant Major while Katchemu had remained a constable.

'Good evening, sir,' he greeted me politely. Then he turned and shook Katchemu warmly by the hand. As I moved slowly off I leaned over and called to him.

'Sergeant Major.'

'Sir,' he turned sharply.

I pointed to Katchemu. 'Try and keep him out of trouble will you?' For a moment the Sergeant Major's usually happy face looked miserable.

'I'll try sir.' Then he shrugged his large shoulders dejectedly. 'But then I always try.'

As I left I heard, even above the roar of the engine, Katchemu's laughter boom out across the compound.

Poor old Josiah, I grinned to myself. He's going to have trouble tonight.

Half an hour later I walked through the doorway of the mess, to stand blinking in the light of a small room filled with forty or so people, all dressed in shorts and open-necked shirts, their jackets lying discarded about the room. Over in the corner a man was pounding away on the piano while a group gathered around him were singing out of tune and beating the rhythm with their beer mugs.

Peter noticed me and, using his enormous bulk, he waded through the crowd, a grin of relief spreading across his good-natured face.

'Thank Christ you've arrived,' he shouted pumping me on the back. Then he nodded towards the milling crowd. 'The natives were just getting restless – another few minutes and they would have come and got you.'

The Member in Charge, his face even redder than usual, came weaving his way towards me. 'Good to see you,' he shouted above the noise. 'Damn fine party.'

'Bill,' I shouted, 'there is something I want to tell you. This afternoon . . .' Someone was tugging at my elbow and people bumped between us. He gave me a lopsided grin as he neatly relieved a passing waiter of a glass of beer.

'It's no good, Terick. Wouldn't understand now anyway. Try me to morrow. Cheers.' He raised the glass to his lips. Then he turned a little unsteadily on his feet and, summoning all his powers of concentration, he weaved his shaky way back to the corner, where he resumed a heated argument with his best friend and greatest rival, the District Commissioner.

Andrew, one of the farm managers, was standing on the bar reciting 'Eskimo Nell' to an enthusiastic audience. Suddenly he spotted me.

'He's arrived,' he shouted. 'There he is. Somebody get the man a beer.' People crowded round. Someone pushed a beer into my hands and I was swept up into a sea of boisterous faces.

Katchemu had just finished his second gallon of beer. He placed the empty jerry-can on the sand while his bloodshot eyes roamed the compound. The fire was stacked high, reaching up into the night. The lone drummer was joined by two more. They sat cross-legged with their beer under a mopani tree at the edge of the circle, the hollow hypnotic beat of their drums gradually filling the air as the alcohol warmed their rhythm.

Katchemu felt good. The second gallon of seven-day beer mixed with illicit sips of kachasu made the whole world seem good. He gave a loud satisfied burp and sat back, letting the rhythm from the drums eat into his brain. Gradually the laughter and talk from the others faded, giving way to the thudding, throbbing message from the drums. It filled his mind, his soul, his body. Sweat sprang out in beads across his face. He felt his heart beat to their rhythm. He felt their power flood into his muscles and he flexed them. He had never felt so strong before. His eyes grew redder as they opened wider, rolling like two red beacons in the night. The blood in his veins seemed to turn to fire and it tingled and pulsed through his body.

Now his mind was throbbing with the drums, bursting in great red stars against his skull, pleading for room. He felt his hair rise on his scalp and he sprang snarling to his feet, a deep low growl rising in his throat. The drummers saw him standing alone on the white sand in the path of the full moon, his head, neck and shoulders shaking in time to their beat, his hands clenching and unclenching like two mighty vices by his sides. They nodded to each other and then increased their rhythm.

The first one started, while the others continued their slow hypnotic throb. His hands began to move faster and faster and faster until they reached a blur across the stretched skin of his drum. A new sound rent the air. The others followed suit. One by one they speeded up, shattering the night with the sounds of their drumming. They held it for a second then the first one slowed, then the second, then the third. Great drops of blood mingled with sweat oozed from under their fingernails.

The drums resumed their slow hypnotic throb. They had caught a soul in passing and now they would make him dance. Katchemu stood rocking on his feet. The first shattering message of the drums had flashed through his brain. 'Fight,' they said. 'Blood,' they said. 'Red flowing blood.' He could almost feel his mighty fist crashing through another man's skull and his low animal growl turned into a mighty yell. It was still echoing round the compound when the drums changed their message.

'Now,' they said, 'dance, Katchemu, dance, let my rhythm take your feet, follow me, follow me. Dance the dance of a warrior, like your grandfather did before his fire. And look, the women watch. See that one running her tongue across her lips, her face shining with sweat. This was how they watched your grandfather. There will be time for her later. But now,

Katchemu, feel your manhood burn within you. Dance Katchemu. Dance as you have never danced before.'

Katchemu stood six feet five upon the sand. His muscles rippling up his arms across his back and down his thighs. He felt his stomach harden. Then, with a yell he tore his thick khaki shirt from the bottom to the neck and tossed it to the ground. He did the same with his trousers, kicking them away to stand stark naked in the moonlight, feeling the night wind cool his tingling body.

The drummers slowly increased their beat and Katchemu began to dance, slowly at first, holding his arms above his head, his knees and ankles close together. He danced on his heels, swaying his massive body from side to side, leaving a snake-like trail across the moonlit sand. The drummers increased their tempo and with them Katchemu. He danced once slowly round the fire, proud of his manhood, his lips parted, his breath coming hard and fast, while the sweat ran in rivers down his body despite the cooling wind.

As he began his second circuit he took a wider course and found Isaac, one of the batmen, cowering in his way. Katchemu was not aware that it was Isaac. All he saw through his bloodshot eyes was a red object squatting in his path. He didn't break the rhythm. He couldn't, for the drummers held him fast. He reached out, still dancing, took Isaac by the scruff of his neck and his trouser seat, and whirling him above his head, threw him away. Isaac bounced against a tree some ten feet farther on and fell back in Katchemu's path. This time he buried his head in his hands and lay still, for Isaac was a little man and he was afraid that if he moved he might offend Katchemu.

The first drummer, then the second, then the third, increased their tempo. Their hands began to fly over the skins. The people around the circle started chanting to the time. The chanting of the people and the throbbing of the drums grew louder, louder, louder. The noise was deafening. Katchemu began to gyrate faster and faster. His arms, legs and head became a blur. He danced right over Isaac, his foot landing squarely on Isaac's head pushing it deep into the sand. Isaac never made a sound. When Katchemu had passed he crawled to safety, spitting out the blood and sand that had collected in his mouth.

The drums reached their crescendo. They held it for a moment, the drummers bathed in sweat, their mouths and eyes wide open, gasping, straining, blood seeping from their bruised fingers staining their skins. Katchemu became a whirling cloud of dust, his lungs sobbing for breath. Then the drummers stopped. The crowd stopped. Katchemu stopped as though paralysed. For a moment there was silence. Then Katchemu raised his naked shining body to its full height. He threw out his chest inflating his lungs to their fullest capacity. 'Ah-eeee-ya-a-a-a-ha!' Some long-forgotten war-cry of his people rang out across the compound, far, far, louder than any of the drums. Then he fell flat on his face on the white moonlit sand. Katchemu's dance was over.

CHAPTER SEVEN

In the mess the party was in full swing. As the beer flowed faster the laughter grew louder. Cigarette smoke hung like a mist in the air. The Member in Charge was playing leap-frog with the District Commissioner, and the game of bottles in the corner had been reduced to everyone shouting 'No!' because they were too drunk to count any more.

An argument had broken out by the piano as to whether the singers would give a rendering of *Sarie Marais* or *Danny Boy*. Sean was leading the Irish contingent and the pianist's head swung from side to side as he nervously played a few notes from each, then stopped hastily when threatened by the rival faction.

Suddenly Peter came pushing his way towards me, dragging Sean along by the arm.

'Terick,' he shouted, 'this bloody leprechaun reckons we'll sort it out with a game of Bok-Bok. I'm leading the Rhodesians, you're leading the British.' He moved away to collect his team.

'So it's a leprechaun I am?' Sean yelled indignantly after him. 'Well, I'm saying, if it hadn't been for us civilizing you, you'd still be wearing grass skirts and a bone through your noses. Now what do you think of that?'

But Peter was too far away and the effect was lost.

'Ah well,' Sean said meditatively. 'Trouble with him is that he doesn't know a good tune when he hears one.'

'What in the hell did you want to do that for?' I groaned. 'Do you want me to get married with a broken back or something?'

Sean patted me confidently on the shoulder. 'We'll pulverize them, Terick boy,' he said cheerfully. 'We'll pulverize them. Just you wait and see.'

Peter won the toss, so we scrummed down against the wall. The Member in Charge and the District Commissioner took opposite sides as usual, while Sean cast aspersions on Peter's musical background from the safety of the scrum.

'Hey,' I shouted, 'no coming down feet first.'

'OK,' Peter answered. 'You ready?' Then he grinned.

One by one they came running down the room, taking off some five feet from the scrum to come crashing down on our backs. The scrum groaned and swore and wheeled and tossed, but it managed to hold up. And one by one they climbed off, disappointed men.

It was Peter's turn. He hummed a few bars of *Sarie Marais* to himself as he measured Sean's position in the scrum. Then he came hurtling down the room, the floor vibrating to his running footsteps. A moment's silence as he launched himself into the air, then Peter struck.

My God! He'd missed his aim. Two hundred and twenty pounds of solid muscle and bone, and he'd landed right on me. The air hissed out from between my teeth like a punctured balloon and I began to sag.

'He's down!' they yelled.

'He's not!' yelled the Member in Charge, holding me up; brightly-coloured stars were swimming before my glazed eyes.

'He's hurt,' they howled.

'He's not,' yelled the Member in Charge.

'My back,' I whistled to no one in particular. 'It's broken!'

'He says he's feeling fine,' yelled the Member in Charge.

'Oh!' said the crowd, disappointed.

'My back,' I whistled feebly again, determined to be heard. 'It's broken!'

' 'Course it's not,' the Member in Charge said in his rough, kindly manner, binding me down. 'It's only bent a bit – that's all.'

I whistled aimlessly, lost for words.

'Nothing to worry about now,' Sean whispered encouragingly to the scrum.

'They've only got the District Commissioner left and he's nothing but an old bag of wind and beer,' the Member in Charge added loudly, and the District Commissioner heard him.

Now the District Commissioner was a man with thirty years' experience. You might even say that he was an expert in these matters. He ran lightly down the room and took off gracefully into the air. He seemed to hang suspended for a moment. Then he came plummeting down hard upon the Member in Charge's neck.

The Member in Charge's head snapped forward. He began to buckle at the knees. It was too late to save him and the whole scrum swayed, then collapsed into a tangled heap on top of him. The opposition were delighted. They rushed up to congratulate the District Commissioner while Peter did a little dance for joy on Sean's head.

Slowly, painfully, we extracted ourselves, the Member in Charge being the last to rise. His nose was bleeding profusely, the impact having driven it into the floor. His eyes spoke of murder whenever he looked at the District Commissioner.

While the opposition was scrumming down we moved over to the bar to plan our revenge. The Member in Charge drank two double whiskies straight off, because, as he claimed, he had lost a lot of blood.

Then one by one we launched ourselves against the opposition. One by one we failed. I dropped from a dizzy height straight between Peter's shoulders and only hurt my behind. The situation was getting desperate. Sean swore that he could hear them all humming *Sarie Marais*.

The Member in Charge wove his way up to the start line, the whisky mingled with revenge burning in his eyes. He rubbed his shoes on the polished floor to obtain a better grip. One – two – three, and he was off, thundering down the room with every muscle straining for the last ounce of speed. With a mighty heave he was about to launch himself into the air, when he tripped on the marker cushion by the start line. He gave a startled yelp as he turned from the perpendicular through ninety degrees to the horizontal and flew the last five feet like a dart, some two feet above the floor, his head and shoulders piercing deep into the rear ranks of the startled scrum while his feet remained twitching at the ceiling.

The whole scrum, under his impetus, launched itself against the wall, and the air was filled with the sounds of crashing heads, As the scrum reeled back Sean made his run. He took off and clutched the rafters. Once there he pulled himself up to the roof and with a look of pure joy on his face – let go. It was too much for the already waiting scrum. With a loud crack and a universal groan they subsided into a tangled heap on the floor.

I recognized the Member in Charge by his bright yellow socks and we pulled him out from underneath a mass of groaning bodies.

'Sheer genius,' we assured him. 'Took them completely by surprise.' But the Member in Charge ignored us. For a few moments he sat, his head on one side, staring into space. Then suddenly he whispered.

'My neck – it's broken. I've broken my ruddy neck.'

' 'Course it's not,' I said in my rough, kindly manner, wriggling it around. 'It's only twisted a bit – that's all.'

41

When most of the bodies had been cleared away we realized that they had suffered one casualty. The District Commissioner had broken his collar-bone, and was lying groaning on the floor. We had all gathered around offering suggestions which he ignored, while Sean, being practical, offered whisky which he gratefully accepted. The Member in Charge pushed his way into the circle, an evil grin on his lips and the station first-aid box under his arm.

One of the Member in Charge's pet hobbies was medicine and during the long evenings as he dozed over one of his massive books on the subject, he often wondered if he had missed his vocation. Now, he informed everyone within earshot, if we would lift the patient onto the bar he would use his newly-acquired skill and set the collar-bone himself.

He then sternly forbade the administering of any more whisky as being detrimental to the patient and in any case wasted on such a person. Instead, he relieved Sean of the bottle and helped himself to a few generous swigs, saying, as he wiped his bloody nose and glared at the District Commissioner, that it would help to steady his shaky hands.

By this time the District Commissioner had opened his eyes, finding himself stretched out on the bar. His gaze travelled wildly across the Member in Charge's face, from his bleeding nose down to the little white box tucked under his arm and marked 'First Aid'.

'Oh no,' he breathed and turned a shade whiter.

The Member in Charge ignored him. He turned to his cheering audience and hiccupped.

'Gentlemen!' he shouted, 'Gentlemen, your attention please! I feel that we should start this operation by giving the patient some small injection. To – ah – put him in the mood, so to speak.'

There came a wave of wild cheering as every one agreed.

'However,' continued the Member in Charge holding up his arms for silence, 'as I can only find snake-bite serum in this outfit, I propose to give him some of that.'

Some offered to hold the District Commissioner down, while the others howled their approval.

The Member in Charge gravely acknowledged the applause with a small bow. Then, dabbing his handkerchief to his nose he turned to his patient.

But the patient was gone. He had sobered up sufficiently and was crawling across the room towards the door as fast as he could, yelling loudly for a doctor. At first the Member in Charge was hurt. Then indignantly he gave orders for the District Commissioner to be collected and returned immediately to his rightful place on the operating table.

A hilarious game of 'Hunt the District Commissioner' began. His exit was cut off and he was heading for the shelter of the tables, when someone furiously began to ring the station alarm bell.

CHAPTER EIGHT

THE urgent clanging of the alarm bell echoed far out into the bush. Everyone froze, their surprised faces open-mouthed, waiting for the laughter that never came. The Member in Charge, who had the knack of sobering up in an emergency, was the first to move.

'Sean, Andrew,' he whispered, 'turn down the lamps. The rest of you get down.'

In an instant the room was dark and we crouched beneath the nearest cover. Then again the Member in Charge's voice cut across the silence of the room.

'Those nearest the windows look out, but don't show your heads.'

The reply came back. 'No one moving in the grounds sir, but there's a hell of a commotion going on over at the station.'

'Can you see the bell?'

I heard someone shifting his position. 'No, sir, not from here.'

'Can anyone see who's ringing that bloody bell?'

'You can't see it from the mess, sir,' Sean said quietly.

'Peter,' the Member in Charge called into the darkness. 'Go and see what's happening. The rest of you stay where you are.'

A shadowy figure detached itself from behind the bar and headed for the window.

'Go carefully,' the Member in Charge called after him.

You could almost see Peter's answering grin in the darkness. 'Too bloody true I will sir.' Then he was gone and the curtains flapped behind him.

I listened for his footsteps on the gravel, but I heard nothing. Any form of civilization made Peter awkward, but in the bush he could move like a shadow flitting from cover to cover. He had recently returned from a six months' stint in the Zambezi Valley, where he had lived in a cave like an animal in an area so harsh and arid that even the local tribesmen could not survive in it. His only contact with the outside world, while he watched a water-hole for signs of terrorist infiltration, was a two-way radio.

I leaned over to the Member in Charge who was crouching near me. 'Why the panic? I thought you said there were no terrorists in the area.'

'Terick,' he replied grimly, 'I don't care what sort of idiot I make of myself. I intend to live to a ripe old age and I'm not taking any bloody fool chances now.'

Suddenly the bell stopped ringing. Then I heard the sound of running footsteps and Peter came bursting through the door. He paused, panting, in the centre of the room. 'It's Sally, a runner's just come. Terick,' he called into the darkness, 'where are you?'

'Over here,' I stood up.

He turned in the direction of my voice. 'She's been hurt,' he panted. 'Out by your farm.'

My head spun and I clutched at the table for support. Then a wave of icy calm cleared my brain. 'Badly?' I asked quietly.

'No one knows,' came the reply. 'A runner carried the news

from your compound and it came down the line from there.'

'Terrorists?' the Member in Charge asked.

'They think so,' Peter said softly, speaking in my direction. 'But we've got the news fifth-hand. No one knows for sure,' he ended helplessly.

The Member in Charge stood up. 'All regulars get your kit and be by the Land Rovers in three minutes,' he ordered. 'Peter, it's Mike on first reserve isn't it?'

'Yes, sir.'

'Well he'll have to stay on the station. Tell him to get the armoury open and issue arms.' Then he turned to the waiting crowd. Someone had lit the lamps and the shadows flickered over their hard brown faces. 'You're all Police Reserves.' It was a statement not a question. 'Go to the armoury and draw weapons. You'll have to use your own transport, sort it out amongst yourselves. Who's the senior man amongst you?'

Andrew stepped forward. 'I suppose I am.'

'Well you see to it,' the Member in Charge snapped.

The Member in Charge's batman appeared bringing his riot blues and he changed in the nearly deserted mess.

'Terick,' he turned to me, 'you'll come with us?' he asked softly.

My hands were clenched by my sides. I didn't feel any pain or fear. I just felt numb inside.

'I'm coming,' I said quietly.

'So am I,' the District Commissioner said, but he winced as he levered himself up against the wall.

'No. I'll make arrangements for you to be taken into hospital and get that bone set. If it is terrorists,' the Member in Charge said, 'we'll both have our work cut out.'

The District Commissioner nodded, more to himself than to the Member in Charge, and lapsed into silence against the wall.

As I made my way over to the Land Rovers I could hear the Member in Charge issuing last-minute instructions on radio procedure to Mike.

'We'll use Channel C,' he was saying. 'If the information

is positive I'll use the code word Starlight. Nothing else. Got it?'

Mike nodded.

'Then you confirm with the code word Sundown. That's all. Don't say anything else. You can't be sure who's listening these days. If it is positive, phone District Headquarters immediately. Tell them that I'll contact them as soon as I can. Then impose a complete security clamp-down. We won't want the news getting out for as long as possible.'

If the information was positive. I shook my head wearily. It had been a long night. Perhaps I was lying under a table somewhere, dead drunk and dreaming.

The African constables came streaming in from their quarters and from the direction of the compound in answer to the bell, doing up their tunics as they ran.

Katchemu leapt the low wire fence surrounding the station and came running towards me dressed only in a pair of tattered shorts.

'Mambo,' he panted, 'is it true? The Madam's hurt?'

I nodded.

'Who?' he demanded.

'I don't know yet.'

He wiped his sweaty hands on the seat of his shorts and grabbing a three-foot baton climbed into the truck.

Peter jumped into the driver's seat. 'Here,' he said, handing me a rifle and a bulging pouch of ammunition. 'With a bit of luck you might need this.'

The Member in Charge stood on the step clutching the roof-rack for support, a Sterling gun slung over his shoulder.

'Channel C, radio silence,' he shouted along the waiting line of Land Rovers. One by one they flashed their headlights to show that they had heard. Then he swung himself into the truck beside Peter.

The air was filled with the sullen roar of engines as the trucks started up. Then we rumbled off at the head of the convoy. I glanced out of the rear window. Through the wire mesh of the riot screens I could see Andrew following in the next truck. Close behind him followed the grey menacing shapes of six other Land Rovers, heeling over as they took the sharp corner at the entrance of the station, the barrels of the rifles in their gun-racks glinting in the lights of the truck behind.

Peter pushed the accelerator to the floor and the laden truck groaned up to its maximum speed, bumping and swaying along the rutted sandy road.

The interior of the truck was dark except for the faint blur of the dashboard lights. Behind me sat Katchemu with the other African constables clutching their weapons, their big frames hunched up close together, rocking to the motion of the truck. The Member in Charge and Peter sat hunched in their seats staring out onto the road ahead. No one spoke, each one's face reflecting the mounting tension.

I felt a dull hurting pain start deep inside me. Suddenly I needed to be alone. I pushed open the hatch above me and stood on the seat, my head and shoulders appearing above the roof of the truck.

Regiments of dark cloud were drawn up against the sky. Silent forks of lightning flashed between them as though some gigantic supernatural battle was taking place. High above it all rode the full moon, filling the patches and flooding the bush with bursts of pale yellow light.

The warm humid air buffeted against my face, clearing the alcohol from my brain. Then I began to make excuses to myself, reasoning out the impression that Sally was hurt.

Peter leaned forward, glancing up at the lightning flashing amongst the clouds. 'It's only an electrical storm now,' he yelled to the Member in Charge. Then he sniffed at the air. 'But I'm telling you there's rain coming. It'll wash out any tracks.'

As if to bear out his words a distant rumble of thunder, like a mountain moving, came wafting on the wind. The Member in Charge nodded worriedly and searched in his pocket for his pipe.

'After all,' I told myself, 'any message that's come fifth-hand is bound to be unreliable. Probably her car has run out of petrol or her mare has run off. Probably she's sitting in my compound now over a warm fire waiting for me to come and collect her.' I gritted my teeth. Provided that nothing had happened to her I'd beat hell out of her behind when I got there. This was the second time she'd done this to me today.

The pain had died to just a nagging doubt as we swung off the road onto the track that led round the Devil's Playground to my farm. I searched the racing sand before me, yellow in the truck headlights, for signs of tyre prints, but there was nothing. The sand was virgin, smoothed by the wind. We skidded around an outlying crop of rocks and came to the last stretch a mile and a half from the farm. The track joined the path leading through the vlei from the rocks, and petered out. Just a few hours before we had cantered along this path, laughing and singing and so very much in love. Behind me the lights from the other trucks flashed against the skyline.

We breasted a small hillock and began the long run down towards the dam. The moon came out from behind the dark clouds and I searched for the cottage. A menacing grumble of distant thunder hung in the air. There, I could see it, nestling small as a toy against the darkened back-drop of the huge kopje. Something was wrong. My heart seemed to slow, then I heard its pumping ringing in my ears. Small shoots of red flame were licking over the thatched roof. A thin white spiral of smoke rose slowly up into the darkened sky. Then the moon went behind the clouds. All I could see were the little pin-pricks of red flame, like cigarette ends glowing in the dark.

'Oh God,' I groaned to myself out loud. 'Let her be all right. Please God,' I prayed looking up into the sky. 'Please. If the farm's destroyed I'll build another. If we've lost everything, I'll start again. But if she's dead. Oh God, I've got no family. I've got nothing in the world but her.' I banged on the roof with my clenched fist so hard that I felt the skin over my knuckles break and the warm blood trickled along my fingers.

The Member in Charge looked up.

'Faster!' I yelled, 'Faster! The farm's on fire!'

He nodded for he had seen the flames too and his face looked drawn and old.

The engine screamed as the truck lurched over the anthills, all four wheels spinning to come crashing down again on the path. Inside the African constables were clinging to the gun-racks for support. Several of their helmets were rolling loose on the floor. Katchemu sat immovable like a rock, one of his great hands clutching the back of the seat like a vice. He looked up at me and said nothing. But his eyes told me that he had seen the fire too.

We were level with the dam now and I could see the flames clearly. The cottage was nearly gutted. One of the walls fell crashing to the ground. Perhaps, I hoped desperately, perhaps she felt cold when she got there and lit a fire. We both loved log fires. Perhaps somehow she set the cottage alight. As if to verify the excuse I began to shiver with cold even though the night was warm.

The truck was nearing the house now. I searched desperately but couldn't see her. The moon had gone back behind the clouds. There ... there suddenly in the red light of the fire I could see three bodies lying on the ground some distance apart. The truck screeched to a halt. I could feel the heat from the fire against my skin.

'Oh God,' I shouted desperately to the sky. 'Please let me speak to her before she dies. Please God don't let her die alone.'

I swung myself onto the roof of the truck and jumped off, stumbling as I hit the ground for I had started to run in mid-air. Then I ran wildly towards the first body.

It was one of the boys from my compound. I leapt over him. Behind me I could hear the others running too. I ran towards the second body, another African. It was old Joseph, lying face down in his blood.

'The bastards. Oh God, the bastards,' I choked as I skirted his body.

I paused searching for the third body, the blood pounding in my head, my lungs gasping for breath. There, I saw it, lying on a patch of white sand nearest the cottage. I ran towards it, stumbling over the tall tussocks of bush-grass. Then the moon came out from behind the clouds, flooding the earth with its cold, white light.

'It's Sally, oh my God, it's Sally, it's Sally.'

I put on a last burst of speed, running wildly as my legs weakened under me. I tripped and fell flat on my face skidding along the ground, the sharp stones beneath me tearing my flesh. But I was up in an instant, the blood singing in my ears. I could see her clearly now as she lay stretched out on the ground. I skidded to a stop on my knees beside her.

'Sally!' I shouted, 'Sally!'

But Sally did not answer. She was dead.

CHAPTER NINE

GENTLY I turned her over onto her back. She lay naked, her skin white and cold in the moonlight, a red circle around her scalp where they had cut off her hair. Two streaks of dried tears ran down her dusty cheeks and there were great red gashes across her body where their knives had torn into her. Blood lay drying in pools on the sand beside her.

'Sally,' I whispered. Her glazed eyes were wide open staring at me but she couldn't see me. Footsteps came running up behind me.

'Keep away, damn you.' I shouted. 'Keep away.'

The footsteps stopped, then turned and walked away. I took off my shirt and gently spread it over her. Then, closing her eyes, I cradled her head in my arms.

'Terick,' the Member in Charge shouted, 'I'm coming over.'

I gently lowered her head onto the sand.

'All right,' I said quietly as I rearranged my shirt. 'All right.'

The Member in Charge and Peter came up softly and knelt beside her. They said nothing.

I wouldn't let them touch her. I gently straightened out her legs and crossed her stiffening arms over her chest. Her left hand was clenched tightly, so tightly that there were red weals where her nails had dug into her skin. I prised her fingers open. Inside, resting on her palm, was our engagement ring.

Peter took off his shirt and he handed it to me across her body. The Member in Charge did the same with his and I gently covered her up.

Someone shouted in the distance. I looked up and saw Sally's mare. She caught my scent and whinnied a greeting, then came painfully hobbling towards me. They had slashed her legs just below the fetlock and left her to bleed slowly to death. Someone cocked a rifle and I shouted at him to stop. She was Sally's mare. I'd do it.

I picked up my rifle and walked towards her. There was pain and trust in her great brown eyes and I patted her sweat-stained neck. 'There's my girl,' I said gently, 'you'll be all right now.' She nuzzled her head against my chest to tell me of her pain. Behind her lay a pool of blood for every step she had taken. I scratched her ears. 'You won't feel anything, I promise. And then for you there will be no more pain.'

I took a pace back and cocked my rifle. The mare lifted her head and tried to hobble towards me. The rifle wavered, then I gritted my teeth and pulled the trigger.

There was a sharp crack as the rifle kicked against my shoulder. The mare's legs crumpled under her. I worked the bolt and fired again to make sure. The mare rolled over onto her side, her legs drumming furiously against the sand. Then she lay still.

'That's one more thing they'll pay for,' I said softly to myself.

I walked back to Sally and knelt beside her. I tore a thin strip off my shirt and, fitting it through the ring, I tied it round her neck, placing it so that it lay in the valley between her breasts. I didn't have our wedding ring with me, but I would put it on later.

People were running back and forth, shouting to each other as they set up ropes and tapes to mark the scene. I turned to walk away. I wanted so much to be alone. Before I went, however, I bent to say goodbye, and I thought that I saw her soul leave her body. I smiled. I knew that she would wait for me, though all I saw was her blood and her tears drying on that sand. I looked up as if to follow the flight of her soul. All I saw was the moon, and even she looked sad.

'I love you, Sally,' I called after her into the night. 'I'll always love you.'

CHAPTER TEN

THE Member in Charge walked over to the Land Rover. He climbed inside and closed the door. For a moment he sat in the silence of the cab, his eyes closed, slumped against the seat. Her father had been his best friend and he had watched Sally grow from a child. He was getting old and sometimes lonely as a bachelor. He had no family, so he had loved Sally from a distance as though she were his own.

His hand reached out for the microphone and he tried to speak but his voice caught in his throat and he coughed fiercely to clear it. He gave the station call sign and a voice answered.

'Is that you, Mike?'

'Yes, sir.'

'Well it's Starlight,' the Member in Charge said gruffly. 'You know what to do.'

'Yes, Sundown,' Mike answered dutifully. Then suddenly he asked, 'How's Terick taking it? Tell him I'm sorry. Tell him if there is anything I can do . . .'

'Just shut up and get on with your job,' the Member in Charge cut in fiercely. He put the microphone back in its rest and then he climbed slowly out of the truck.

Mike switched the set onto 'Receive Only' and then he stood staring at the silent radio. 'You bloody callous old bastard,' he said disgustedly. 'You wouldn't know what it feels like. All you've got is a copy of standing orders inside you instead of a heart.' Then he turned and walked off to phone District Headquarters.

Katchemu turned old Joseph over onto his back. Then he rested his great grey head against the old man's chest and listened. There, he could hear it, the faint hesitant beats of the old man's heart. Katchemu sat back on his haunches grunting with satisfaction and felt in his pockets for a flask of muti.

The witch-doctor, who had sold it to him for the sum of ten pounds, had promised that as long as a spark of life remained in a man's body this muti would revive him for a few seconds. Since that day Katchemu had always carried the flask with him, for he knew that, if ever he were killed, he would dearly want enough life to take the man who did it with him.

He uncorked the flask with his teeth and forced a little of the evil-smelling muti down Joseph's throat. After a few seconds the old man started to choke, red bubbles of blood forming on his lips.

'Joseph,' Katchemu said softly, and the old man opened his eyes. 'Tell me quickly, who were the men who killed my Madam?'

The old man's eyes wandered up and found Katchemu's face. 'I'm dying,' he said simply. 'Let me die Katchemu.' Then he turned his face away.

Katchemu was disgusted. He seized Joseph's hair and wrenched his head round.

'Tell me Joseph,' he said fiercely. 'What did they look like, these men who killed my Madam?'

Joseph shook his head. There was terror in his eyes.

'Joseph,' Katchemu whispered in his ear, 'if you don't tell me quickly I will take your head and twist it until you look the wrong way. Also,' he added as a further inducement, 'I will burn your kia, take your wives, defile your daughters and feed your grandchildren to the jackals. All this I will do Joseph.'

There were tears of rage in Katchemu's bloodshot eyes. Joseph saw them. His face was grey and twisted with pain, but he talked though his strength was failing fast.

'One, the leader, was white. He was dressed as a European but he was not a European. He was a spirit. There were others. Africans. They had guns. They came to the compound while I was drinking beer. They said that they would kill me if I did not show them the Mambo's house.'

The old man's fingers plucked at Katchemu's arm. 'I didn't know that the Madam was there,' he said pleadingly, 'I thought the house was empty.'

'Go on,' Katchemu ordered. He forced more muti down Joseph's throat and leant a little closer, for the old man's voice was failing.

'Go on,' he snarled, grasping Joseph's hair.

'The spirit called outside the house. In the night the Madam thought he was a European because of his white skin. She came out. They killed her. Caspar from the compound was with her. He tried to save her but they killed him too. Then they killed me.'

The old man writhed in pain as the last of the muti left his system. Katchemu pinned his shoulders to the ground.

'Where did they go?' he shouted. 'Which way did they go?'

Joseph's voice came from far away as he gasped for breath, choking through the blood that bubbled in his mouth.

'They went to the north,' he whispered, 'but they came in from the haunted rocks.'

Katchemu sat back satisfied, flinging the empty flask aside. Suddenly the old man sat up, clutching Katchemu's arm, his eyes staring wildly at him.

'He said that he's a spirit, Lobengula's spirit risen from the rocks. He says that he'll drive the Europeans from this land.

His eyes are those of a spirit, Katchemu. They could take a man's soul away. And he speaks so softly. His followers ... they call him "The Whispering Death" for none shall hear him coming.'

Suddenly there were tears flowing down the old man's face. 'I was frightened, Katchemu. Tell the Mambo I'm sorry. Only that I am an old man and was frightened ... so frightened of the spirit.'

Katchemu laid the old man, dead, upon the ground.

'Joseph,' he said by way of an epitaph as he stood up, 'you were only a little man, but I,' he tapped his chest, 'I am a big man and therefore not afraid.'

Peter found me sitting on top of the kopje staring out across my lands. I did not hear him coming, only the stone he threw to warn me of his presence.

We sat in silence. Above us the lightning flashed and the thunder rumbled in amongst the heavy black clouds.

'Oh Peter,' I said softly. 'Oh Peter, I wish I could cry. I've been sitting here trying to cry, to break down and sob my heart out. But I can't. I can't, Peter. I've forgotten how to cry.'

A sudden flash of lightning brighter than the rest split the night. With it came a single clash of thunder right above us. Then the rain came pouring down, the cold heavy drops drumming on my naked back and trickling down my face like tears.

We walked slowly down the kopje towards the cottage. The charred wooden rafters which I had spent so many weeks fashioning into place lay buckled to the ground across the broken walls. The brick and timber from the bedroom lay glowing and hissing on the foundations of the nursery that never was. For a while I stood looking at the gutted wreckage of my home. I thought of all the work, the hope and the love that had gone into its building. Now there was nothing ... nothing but the dying embers left.

'You can sell the land and start again,' a voice came from

behind. I turned. Peter, Andrew, Sean and several of the others had gathered.

'Anybody want to buy a dream?' I asked. I turned back to the ruins of my home and said again, softly to myself, 'Anybody want to buy a dream?' But they didn't understand and I walked away.

The Member in Charge found me sitting by Sally's body.

'We found some footprints before the rain washed them away,' he said quickly, trying to take my mind off Sally. 'Look like army boots heading north. They'll be trying to get back to the border. But don't worry,' he said grimly, 'we'll get them. I promise you that.'

I looked up. 'You also said that there were no terrorists in this area,' I snarled.

The Member in Charge's face flushed but he let it go.

'Sally will have to go into town for a post-mortem,' he said softly.

'Why? You can see how she died. You don't need a ruddy doctor to tell you.'

'Terick, you know we've got to get a post-mortem report.'

'All right then, I'll go with her.'

The Member in Charge shook his head. 'We'll take good care of her,' he said kindly. 'You'd better go and tell her grandfather.'

'Oh God,' I thought. 'I'd forgotten all about him. She was all he had too.'

'Do you want her to stay there?' he asked.

'No,' my skin crawled at the thought of her lying on a cold stone slab in a mortuary. 'Will you bring her right back? My boys, too. Their families will want to bury them. And I'll bury Sally on my farm.'

The Member in Charge nodded. 'She'll be back early this evening.'

I found Andrew huddled under a low overhang of rock, trying to shelter from the driving rain until the search started at first light.

'May I borrow your truck?' I asked. 'I'll see that it's returned.'

'Of course.' His hands dived in to his trouser pockets and he threw the keys out to me. 'Keep it as long as you like. Is there anything else I can do?'

The rain began to ease as I went in search of his truck, the thunder moving into the distance. 'In a few minutes the storm will have passed but it'll be too bloody late,' I told myself bitterly. 'They'll have nothing to go on now.'

The whole area was under a sea of churning mud, little storm-streams rushing down the sides of the kopje into the dam in the valley below. The bushmen and tracker dogs would be useless in this. Come first light they would have to start searching blindly for a little band of well-trained men in a thousand miles of bush.

I put the Land Rover into four-wheel drive and began to ease it through the mud when a shout turned my head and I saw Katchemu running after me. I slowed and he leapt into the back. In the dim glow of the dashboard lights he saw my ashen face and shook his head miserably.

'Mambo,' he said softly, 'I'm sad for you and the Madam. I'm sad unto death.' Then he lapsed into silence against the gun-racks.

I parked the truck in the courtyard and began the long climb up the winding stone stairway. As I climbed I wondered what I'd say. How do you tell a sick old man that the last of his family is dead?

The front door was slightly ajar. It creaked as I pushed it open and softly entered the hall. Along the passage a faint light glowed from under the sitting-room door. I walked towards it, my footsteps muffled on the carpet. The old man was in his dressing-gown, sitting by himself in the darkened room in his usual high-backed chair. He looked up from the fire as I entered and waved me to a seat beside his.

'Don't bother to tell me,' he said softly. 'I already know. My boys brought me word.'

He poured two glasses of brandy and handed one to me. It

seemed as though the iron had left his spirit for now his shoulders sagged and his white-capped head was bowed to his chest. As he sat staring into the fire two tears squeezed out from behind his eyelids and trickled slowly down his weatherbeaten face. Suddenly I knew that I loved this proud old man and I wanted to tell him so. I wanted so much to say, 'You still have me. I'm young and I'm strong. Lean on my shoulders old man.' But the words wouldn't come so I leaned across and gently squeezed his arm.

He looked up and he seemed to understand, for he said softly, 'Where shall we bury her?'

'On my land. Under that willow tree by the dam. If that's all right with you.'

He nodded slowly. 'That's a good place.' Then he felt the tracks where the warm tears had turned cold on his cheeks, and ashamed he brushed them away.

I think that he felt more coming and being too old to turn them back, he said softly, 'Terick, I need to be alone for a while.'

I nodded and quietly crossed the room. By the door I paused, for in the dim flickering light of the fire I could see that his head was buried in his hands and his shoulders were gently shaking. I started to speak. Then I thought better of it and I closed the door softly behind me, leaving the old man alone with his sorrow.

The Land Rover skidded to a halt outside the station spewing gravel over the immaculately kept lawn. The Member in Charge climbed out and strode through the Charge Office door. Mike was waiting for him in his office.

'I've cleared the line, sir. The OC's waiting for you.'

The Member in Charge picked up the telephone. 'All right,' he nodded briefly, 'you can leave.'

Mike walked out closing the door behind him.

'Hello, hello,' came a harassed voice on the other end of the line. 'Is that you Bill?'

'Yes, sir.'

'You took a long time coming.'

'I was thirty miles away when I got your call,' the Member in Charge answered shortly.

'Well what's the position?'

'One of my patrol officers',' the Member in Charge paused. 'One of my ex-patrol officers' fiancée was murdered by a group of terrorists at about twenty-three hundred hours, on their farm. They also killed two of his employees and burnt down his house. We've just had a freak thunderstorm and it's washed out all chance of tracks. I'm going to try a wide sweep of the area at first light. Try and pick up fresh ones, though God knows there is not much hope.'

'Well you're going to have to find them, Bill.' The voice at the other end spoke quietly. 'There have been four other outbreaks of terrorism in different parts of the country and we're expecting more terrorists to cross the Zambezi at any moment. CID can't help you.'

For a moment the Member in Charge was silent. 'So it's come has it?'

'Yes. But we can handle it as long as they don't get into the main townships.'

'All right, sir. But I'm going to need at least one helicopter, some tracker dogs and a few bush-men trackers if you can get them for me. Some of the country's pretty rugged round here. And men, sir. I need more men.'

'I'm sorry, Bill,' the voice was firm. 'I can't help you. We're stretched to breaking point as it is. Your area is not so important. You'll just have to manage with your Police Reserves.'

'Sir,' the Member in Charge's voice was hard. 'I've got a responsibility to protect the people in my area. Those terrorists might be anywhere within a radius of seventy miles. They might strike again tonight.'

'Bill, I told you I'm sorry, but there is nothing I can do. If the situation eases I might be able to get help to you in a few days.'

'Very good, sir,' the Member in Charge said slowly. 'I'll do what I can.'

'Good.' The OC's voice was brisker now as though a great

weight had been lifted from his shoulders. 'By the way, this patrol officer. What's his name? The one who's just left the force.'

'Hurndell, sir, Terick Hurndell.'

'What's he like?'

'He's a quiet, easy-going fellow, a bit of a dreamer. But there is a hard streak in him and he loved that girl. She was all he had. I like him. I like him a lot.'

'How's he taking it?'

'Very well sir. In fact he hardly showed any emotion at all.'

'Well you'd better keep him out of it all the same.'

'Yes, sir. I'd already decided to.'

'Good, well that's all then. Keep me informed. Oh, and Bill – the Commissioner asked me to tell you that he has every confidence in you to contain the situation; so have I.'

There came a click as the receiver was replaced on its rest and the line went dead. The Member in Charge slowly replaced his. He stood looking at it for a while. Then he walked across to a wall map on the other side of the office.

I wandered slowly out of the courtyard onto a small path leading down to the dam, my hands in my pockets, my head bent low. On either side the pine trees towered above me, their ghostly branches softly whispering in the warm night wind. Once I heard a rustle and turning back I saw Katchemu following in the distance.

'Go away,' I yelled, and he dropped quietly out of sight.

I sat on the banks of the dam listening to the crickets in the branches and the croak of the bullfrogs in the reeds. Above me the storm had completely cleared, leaving only a few wistful clouds drawn up across the sky like waves. Between them rode a huge yellow moon like a ship on a gentle sea.

'You saw it all,' I thought as I looked up. 'You know how I feel.' Then, with the gentle lapping of the water, I sobbed my heart out.

I sobbed in great choking gasps that racked my chest and swelled in my throat, until the tears which I thought I had lost came welling into my eyes and ran streaming down my cheeks to fall with little splashes into the still waters of the dam. I cried as I had done only once before as a little boy, rocking back and forth upon my heels with my arms clenched tightly round me.

I saw my teardrops making ripples growing wider, ever wider on the glass-like surface of the dam, until they made the moonbeams dance to comfort me across the dark waters. I felt the pain and anger rise within me, until a great red fire of revenge took possession of my soul. Then with the coming of the dawn I fell asleep hunched up on the bank. Katchemu, who had been watching from the shelter of the tall grass stole out and made me comfortable, spreading his shirt over me and collecting a pillow of moss for my head. Then he mounted guard over my sleeping form, nodding to himself as he did so for he was glad that at last the tears had come.

The chair creaked as the Member in Charge leant back, fumbling in his pockets for his pipe. His mind was nearly numb with weariness. The taste of stale alcohol and tobacco lingered in his mouth. He rested his legs against the windowsill and stared with vacant eyes across the bush to where the first faint traces of the coming dawn glowed pale red against the sky from behind the Duvumbera Mountains.

It was only twenty-four hours since last he slept but it seemed more like days. His chin rested on his chest and his eyelids began to flicker in answer to the persistent waves of weariness that battered against his will power. In spite of himself his hard face softened and his mind began to wander to the little cottage that he had bought up in the mountains by a small rushing river, where the trout jumped in the evenings and the grass grew so green, like home. Just one year to his pension . . . just one more year.

The Member in Charge's pipe slipped from his mouth and fell noisily to the floor. He started guiltily and bent to pick it up. 'You're getting old,' he snarled angrily to himself, 'and soft.' Then he thought of the days to come and his face hardened. 'But you're not finished yet.'

Slowly he re-lit his pipe and turned his attention back to the large wall map in front of him, trying to work out where he could place road blocks, patrols, his search patterns and, most important, how he was going to feed and supply all his men once they were swallowed up in the vast expanse of uncharted bush that lay to the north.

All his men. He grunted to himself and, for the twentieth time, he started to count the number of regulars, A-reserves, field reserves and special reserves that he could call on. Anyone who could walk, he decided, would be counted. Then, again for the twentieth time, he studied the map and tried to put himself into the position of the terrorist leader.

Which way would he run? North, it had to be north. He'd done his little act of violence. Now he would head back to the friendly border as fast as his legs could carry him. For a second the Member in Charge considered Terick's theory, then he discarded it. No, to move in any other direction would be committing suicide. Everyone was on the alert. Sooner or later they would bump into one of the patrols or be spotted by the local tribesmen.

And yet – the Member in Charge tried to visualize the terrorist leader, would he take the gamble? Would he try for another farm or terrorize a few isolated compounds and murder the headmen, knowing all the while that his escape was being cut off? The Member in Charge shook his head. No, his food, ammunition and water must be running low. Time was against him. If he wanted any chance of escape he'd have to make his run now. And if he did, which route would he take? Obviously he would try and avoid the populated areas, but rather keep to the thick bush for cover. He would probably make use of the dried up water-courses at night for easier going, and hide up during the day.

The Member in Charge leant back in his chair and drew heavily on his pipe. He did not have enough men to cover both possibilities. He had made his choice, and he hoped to God it was the right one.

Peter, Sean and Mike were outside the station marshalling

the Police Reserves who had already arrived in answer to the general call-out which had been issued earlier that morning.

The Police Reserves did not talk to one another as they stamped around trying to keep warm in the now cold, hard light of dawn. Instead, under their battered bush hats, their faces were set hard and grim. Most of them had known Sally since she was a child, and her godfather and several adopted uncles stood in the crowd. An hour later the last of the Police Reserves had arrived and were formed up under the flags in front of the station.

Peter went to report to the Member in Charge.

'What's their mood like?' the Member in Charge asked.

'Evil,' Peter answered, 'like mine.'

The Member in Charge looked up sharply. 'I didn't ask for your feelings.'

Peter remained stiffly silent.

'Anyway,' the Member in Charge continued, 'you're staying in charge of the station. You can have five constables to help you.'

'Like hell I will,' Peter exploded. 'You know I'm better than any of the others in the bush.'

'Don't shout at me,' the Member in Charge said quietly. 'You received an order. Now obey it.'

He looked up at Peter's face and then he added kindly, 'Peter, you're the senior Patrol Officer. We're short of a Section Officer so you'll have to take his place. I'll be bobbing in and out of the station while I'm directing the search, and I need a man that I can rely on to back me up here, all right?'

'Very good, sir,' Peter said woodenly.

In the back of his mind the Member in Charge knew of other reasons for keeping Peter out of the field. The most important being that Peter was too dangerous and too emotionally involved. In his present state of mind he would make a dedicated terrorist hunter but a very bad policeman.

'By the way,' he asked, still half-occupied with his thoughts, 'is Terick out there?'

'No, sir. I don't know where he's got to.'

The Member in Charge felt relieved. He didn't want

Terick along, for the same reason. But all the same he felt a little worried by his absence.

'Sir.' Peter drew his attention. 'I'd like to go to Sally's funeral this evening. Andrew will stand in for me until I get back.'

The Member in Charge nodded. 'All right but make yourself easily available in case I should need you in a hurry.'

'Thank you, sir. Is that all?' Peter moved towards the door. The Member in Charge smiled. Discipline sat heavily on Peter's broad shoulders.

'Are many people going to the funeral?' he asked quietly.

'No, sir,' Peter said, unbending a little. 'As far as I can gather it's a family affair. Just the old man, Terick and me.'

'I thought so,' the Member in Charge said softly. 'Keep an eye on Terick and the old man for me, and let me know how they're taking it.'

'I'll do that,' Peter said earnestly. 'I haven't seen the old man yet but, I'm telling you, I'm dead worried about Terick.'

'So am I,' the Member in Charge said. Then, again, softly to himself, he said, 'So am I.'

'Shall I tell them that you're coming out, sir?'

'Yes,' the Member in Charge looked up. 'Tell them I'm coming just now.'

Peter walked out into the crisp clean air of the early morning. 'He'll be coming just now,' he told the impatient Police Reserves. Then he went off to choose the African constables who would remain with him.

The Member in Charge stood on the steps of the Charge Office facing the Police Reserves. His gaze swept down their irregular lines taking in their hard brown faces, their cold angry eyes. They dressed as they chose, in the faded browns and greens of camouflage saved over from the war, or in old sweat-stained bush jackets, and a sprinkling of those in blue riot dress showed here and there. Each one's belt bulged with ammunition and each one clutched his rifle to him as though it were his wife. Every pair of eyes said, 'It could have been my family. It could have been my farm.' A savage mood of anger and revenge hung in their impatient silence.

The Member in Charge turned to Peter who was standing beside him. 'I don't know if they'll frighten the terrorists,' he said uneasily, 'but my God they frighten me.' His gaze travelled across to the larger African contingent on the other side, all standing stiffly to attention, immaculate in their starched riot dress. He shook his head in wonder for they had all turned out, and the Sergeant Major, whose special charges they were, swelled with pride as he stood before them.

'Gentlemen,' the Member in Charge lifted his voice, 'by now you will have received your instructions and been allotted your search areas. But I want to make something very clear to you before you leave.' The Member in Charge paused while the Sergeant Major translated his every word in a parade ground bellow for the benefit of the African Police Reserves.

'Now I know that you've all known Sally since she was a little girl. And I know that several of you have kept a fatherly eye on her since her parents died. I also know,' the Member in Charge shouted above the murmuring crowd, 'that Terick and the old man are very popular in the district. But I want to make it clear that you are Police Reserves, not some posse out of a Wild West film. From now on you have the same responsibilities and you're under the same discipline as the regulars. You'll be operating under difficult conditions, but your sole objective is to maintain the law throughout the district. Nothing more. Do I make myself absolutely clear? You are not here to extract personal vengeance.'

The angry murmuring from the Police Reserves escalated against the Member in Charge's tirade.

'It's all right for you,' someone shouted. 'You haven't got a wife and family. You don't know how it feels.'

The Member in Charge was afraid that they might melt away before his eyes. Essentially these men were loners, choosing the isolated existence of a farm where they could pit their individual strengths against the elements, rather than the disciplined existence of a city. All the while they lived against the cruel backdrop of Africa where, just a few years ago, only the strong survived and justice was in action not in words. True, centuries of civilization had taught them to respect the law, but at times like this, way out in the bush, their veneer of civilization lay very thin. The Member in Charge knew this. He knew that he had to hold them by the sheer force of his personality and their embodied respect of the law he represented.

He caught a glimpse of the speaker. 'Tom,' he called, 'I've lived with Terick for two years. I introduced him to Sally. I tell you, man, I know just how you feel.' He turned back to the crowd. 'But don't you see, you're behaving just as they want you to. These isolated acts of terrorism are designed to make you lose your heads. They know they can't frighten you out, so they're hoping that they can get you so angry that you'll march into a reserve and start blasting away at anything you see. If you do this you'll have lost everything that has taken us years to achieve, the rule of law and,' he glanced over at the African Police Reserves, 'the support of the Africans. Do you want to be responsible for changing all that?' the Member in Charge shouted.

There was a long silence.

'While you're in the bush,' he continued, 'you'll account for every round of ammunition that you use. Heaven help you if you kill an innocent man. Remember, if you're not sure, don't shoot. Lastly, I want to impress upon you that I'll deal ruthlessly with any man who takes the law into his own hands.'

'All right, Bill, all right,' someone shouted from the crowd. 'You can stop threatening us. We're with you.'

'But look, Bill,' a man in a camouflage jacket standing in the front row said, 'here we are going after well-trained terrorists, all probably armed with machine guns, and you're stuffing us with regulations. Hell, man, what do you expect us to do? Stand up in the bush, wave our bloody hats and yell "Hey, you over there, are you a terrorist?" to a man who's probably hiding a machine gun up his jacket?'

'No,' the Member in Charge said slowly, 'I'm not asking

you to commit suicide. All I'm saying is that our job is to protect the innocent as well as catch the guilty. Tell me,' he continued softly, looking at the man in the camouflage jacket, 'how would you feel if you killed some old bush man, just because he happened to stray across your path?'

The man in the camouflage jacket did not answer. He looked at the ground and kicked apologetically at a stone.

'Now,' thought the Member in Charge, 'is the time to end this parade.'

'There is just one last thing, Bill.' Ian MacFarlane, the senior section leader, stepped forward from the crowd. He was a retired colonel and his voice held the quiet authority of a man used to command. 'When can we expect reinforcements to arrive?'

The Member in Charge braced himself. Then he shook his head. 'There aren't going to be any, Ian – at least not for a couple of days.'

'Why?'

'There aren't enough men to go round and we're the last on the list.'

'But that's madness. They might have slipped through our fingers by that time.'

'No they won't, Ian,' the Member in Charge said softly.

The Police Reserves saw an expression of grim certainty on his face and they believed him.

CHAPTER ELEVEN

THE prisoner turned away from the window. 'May I have that glass of water now?'

The warder reached down for a Thermos flask that lay by his side. 'You can have some tea if you like, it's good and strong.'

'What time is it?'

The warder glanced at his watch. 'Two a.m. Here,' he said feverishly, 'you'd better hurry.'

The prisoner's face was pale and drawn from the agony of reliving what had been a memory.

'I'm sorry about your missus,' the warder said softly.

CHAPTER TWELVE

I AWOKE stiff and cramped. The smell of woodsmoke turned my head and I saw Katchemu cooking fish which he had caught from the dam. As I walked over to him he swiftly seized one from the fire and dipped it into the water. With a hiss of steam the baked clay covering fell away and he handed me the fish rolled in leaves.

'Eat,' he said, as I handed him back his shirt.

'Sailor?' I asked.

'Boss Peter is looking after him at the station.'

I squatted beside him looking into the water. 'Katchemu,' I said slowly, 'last night I thought of my Madam and my farm. Now I have this anger burning in my belly, like a fire. Only those men's blood can put it out.' I looked up. 'Will you come with me, Katchemu?'

'Oh Mambo,' Katchemu said softly. 'I will follow you unto death. She was my Madam and it was my farm too.' He sat back on his haunches. His lips drew a thin line across his darkened gums and his bloodshot eyes glowed with rage. 'We'll go hunting, you and I, my Mambo. And when we catch these men we will do to them what they did to the Madam, only more so,' he breathed.

For a while we sat in silence. The pact was made. Then I asked hopelessly, 'Katchemu, how are we going to hunt these men if we don't even know where to look for their trail?'

Katchemu shrugged his shoulders. 'Last night I spoke with the old man, Joseph, before he died. He told me that these men went to the north. But they came from the haunted rocks. He also said that the leader was white. But he was not a European.'

'An albino?' I asked looking up.

Katchemu nodded. 'Old Joseph said he was a spirit. But then old Joseph was a fool. Anyway,' he growled, 'we will see if he dies when we kill him.'

'This man,' I prompted, 'does he claim that he's the spirit of Lobengula?'

Katchemu nodded again, wondering how I knew. Then suddenly he understood. 'The mad woman,' he said excitedly, 'the one who came to the camp that night. This is the man?'

'And the rocks Katchemu. Old Joseph said that he came from the rocks. He's got his base camp in there somewhere.'

Katchemu shook his head. 'Mambo, why should he go back to the rocks. Surely he'll be running now, trying to get away. Besides, old Joseph was right. I saw the tracks before the rain came. They were heading north.'

I sat back staring out across the dam. 'I know he's still here Katchemu. I can feel him. Besides, why should he go to so much trouble to convince the people that he is Lobengula's spirit if he is only going to kill once and then run away? No,' I shook my head, 'he's after bigger things.'

'Mambo, if you're right,' Katchemu groaned, 'if he is in the rocks, how are we going to find him?'

I shrugged my shoulders helplessly. 'I don't know.'

'It would take an army to search every kopje and every cave in that vast wilderness.'

'If only old Joseph were still alive,' Katchemu said softly, breaking the silence, 'perhaps he could have told us.'

I scrambled to my feet. 'That's it, Katchemu. The mad woman. She's still alive. She might be able to tell us.'

Katchemu shook his head doubtfully. 'Not that one Mambo. She's too mad.'

'We've got to try. She's our only chance.'

The mad woman lived alone in a small ramshackle mud and thatched hut set well away from the rest of her village in the reserve bordering the Devil's Playground.

'Stop here, Mambo,' Katchemu motioned me to the side of the track. 'If she hears us coming she'll run away.'

I parked the Land Rover outside the village and we walked silently through the bush to her hut. By the door we paused, listening to the faint sounds of her moving within. Katchemu's hand stole out and softly tried the latch. It was bolted. He knocked on the door.

'Mad woman,' he said softly, 'it is us, the Mambo and me. Let us in so we may talk with you.'

The sounds of movement stopped. There was no reply. Katchemu knocked again, this time louder than before.

'Mad woman, this is Katchemu. Let us in. I won't hurt you.'

There was still no reply. Katchemu seized the latch and rattled the door until the mud walls shook.

'The Mambo and I have come a long way to speak with you,' he shouted indignantly.

The mad woman gave a shriek of wild laughter, but she made no move to open the door. Katchemu never was a patient man. Before I could stop him, he launched a kick against the latch. The bolt burst and the shattered door fell inwards.

'That,' grumbled Katchemu as he stooped to enter the hut, 'is what I should have done first.'

I followed him through the narrow doorway. The mad woman cowered against the farthest corner, gibbering with terror, her arms folded across her face as though to protect her from the shaft of sunlight that penetrated the cold dark gloom of her hut. Suddenly the stench of human dirt and decay filled my nostrils. My stomach heaved. I turned and staggered back towards the door.

'Get her outside,' I choked.

Katchemu caught my arm and held me. 'It's no good. This one's frightened by the daylight. She only goes out after dark.'

'All right,' I nodded, 'leave me for a moment.' I leant against the doorway waiting for my senses to accept the stench and my heaving stomach to subside.

Softly at first, rocking back and forth upon her haunches, the mad woman started to sing. There were no words, just a breathless, eerie whispering sound that sent my spine crawling. Her voice rose and her rocking grew harder until she was flinging herself against the wall, tearing at her face and hair, while bubbles of white saliva ran trickling down her chin. Suddenly she started to scream, her voice rising higher and higher until I thought it would break.

Her madness affected Katchemu. He seized a log of wood and strode towards her. 'Shut up!' he yelled. 'Shut up or I'll kill you!' The scream stopped suddenly as the mad woman looked up and saw Katchemu towering above her. For a moment there was silence as she stared, still open-mouthed, at the heavy log he brandished above his head. Then, whimpering quietly, like a wounded animal she turned her face to the wall.

'Come away Katchemu,' I ordered. 'Don't frighten her any more.'

Katchemu dropped the log. 'She's not that mad,' he said disgustedly. 'She's fooling you. If you're gentle with her she'll never tell you anything.'

'We haven't tried yet. Help me block out the light.'

Together we fitted the broken door back into its frame. Then in the semi-darkness of the hut we sat before the mad woman on the dirty earthen floor. I reached out, trying to reassure her, but she jerked away leaving a strip of rotted clothing in my hands.

'Those men,' I said softly, 'the ones you told us about. They killed my woman. Tell me where they are now. Please tell me.'

The mad woman did not answer.

'You talk to my Mambo,' Katchemu said harshly, 'or I'll split your skull.' His hands reached out for the log.

'Leave her alone,' I said angrily.

Katchemu shrugged his huge shoulders. 'That night she

came to our camp. She could speak then. She's fooling you, Mambo. You're only a European. You don't understand.'

The mad woman turned to me. Silent tears made furrows through the dirt and mud that caked her grey, wrinkled cheeks. She said something in the vernacular.

I turned to Katchemu. 'What did she say?'

'She says that she is frightened of me, that I am an evil man.'

'What's she saying now?'

'She's threatening to put a curse on me,' Katchemu said indignantly. 'Look Mambo. Perhaps if I kill her a little bit she'll tell us.'

'No.'

I took my lighter from my pocket and flicked it. The flame glowed. I flicked it again and again. Then I held it out to her.

'Tell her she can have it if she tells us.'

Katchemu translated. Slowly the mad woman's hand reached out for it and then she started to speak.

'She says she doesn't know where those men are. But there is a special meeting in the rocks tonight. Some of the young men are going. There will be a big ceremony.'

'Where is this place?'

'She says that she doesn't know. Only that it is very full of spirits and there is a special stone.'

I remembered the altar stone and the beaten ground around it. I gave the mad woman the lighter and started to my feet. 'I know the place. Come on.'

The mad woman flicked the lighter and crooned over the dancing flame.

'Perhaps,' Katchemu said wistfully, as we walked towards the Land Rover, 'she'll burn the hut down.'

'We need rifles, food and clothing,' I said, as we drove back towards the farm. 'Did Boss Andrew take the .303 when he collected his Land Rover this morning?'

Katchemu grinned. 'He couldn't find it.'

'Where is it?'

'I've hidden it with the bullets.'

'Do you know how many bullets there are?'

'Sixty, in two pouches,' Katchemu said proudly. 'I stole Boss Peter's as well.'

'I'm going back to the station to pick up some hard rations. I'll bring enough for three days. After that we'll have to manage as best we can. You go up to the house and find me an old bush jacket and some long trousers. Rub patches of mud into them. Then get me a pair of strong boots with thick rubber soles. Make sure the boots are dull and that there are no shiny buttons. Get the same for yourself.'

'When do we leave Mambo?'

'Directly after the funeral.'

'Don't bring the dog with you.'

'Why not?'

'When a dog runs or gets hot it pants. That noise is no good for what we are going to do in the bush, Mambo.'

I parked near the farmhouse. 'Katchemu,' I said suddenly, 'are you afraid of dying?'

Katchemu smiled. He shook his grey head. 'I'm old now, Mambo. Soon I'll die anyway. It's better to die fighting than in a bed surrounded by frightened women. Besides,' he tapped his stomach, 'I have this anger.'

I parked the truck at the back of the station. The atmosphere was one of organized chaos. Constables ran back and forth across the hard square, bearing messages, while Land Rovers screamed in from the field to refuel and then speed on their way.

Cautiously I made my way through the African Police camp to the rear of the stables which, since the disuse of horses, had now been converted into store-rooms. I was about to walk around to the doors when some sixth sense made me check to see that all was clear.

Above me was a small barred window. I reached up and grasping the bars raised myself until I could just see through the dusty window-panes. As I had hoped, both doors were open for easy delivery of supplies to the men in the field. Then something caught my eye. In the bright patch of sunlight by the first door was the distinctive shadow of a constable's helmet. I swore quietly to myself and dropped to the ground. Someone must have put him on guard to stop any pilfering of supplies by the camp labourers.

I drew myself up to check again. The constable's position hadn't changed, but I noticed that his helmet was sloping sharply downwards. For a moment I was puzzled then suddenly I realized that they had been on duty all night. The guard was probably fast asleep.

I moved quietly round to the front. Constable Zacriah, true to his nature, had rested his shoulders against the stable walls and, in the shade of the overhanging roof, dozed off. There was an opinion held by certain sergeants who had dealings with him, that Zacriah was permanently asleep. As they regularly complained to the Member in Charge, he was the laziest, most unreliable constable on the station.

I walked past him and into the store-room. From a pile against one of the walls I took six small cardboard boxes, each containing hard rations for twenty-four hours, and together with other equipment which we needed, I placed them into two field-grey haversacks with dull black painted over their brass buckles. Then, swinging the haversacks over my shoulder, I walked out of the store-room.

No one had seen me. No word of my actions would reach the Member in Charge's suspicious ears. We could still count on forty-eight hours' clear start. I was about to make my way back to the fence when a cough made me start and then turn.

Constable Zacriah slowly opened his sleepy eyes. 'Good luck, Mambo,' he said softly. Then he settled his shoulders against the wall, closed his eyes and went back to sleep.

CHAPTER THIRTEEN

WE buried Sally at sundown, the old man, Peter and I, in a deep grave at the foot of the willow tree by my dam. We covered the grave with heavy rocks and placed wild flowers at her head and her feet.

No, I remembered her wedding ring.

Then we stood for a while, heads bowed, each with our own private prayer. I remember the old man at the head of the grave, his white hair and beard aflame in the sunset, the shadows accentuating the creases of pain in his face.

By the light of a tilley lamp we erected a crude wooden cross carved from the charred rafters of our home. The inscription was simple. It gave the date that she died, and the fact that we loved her.

Then we left.

CHAPTER FOURTEEN

PETER had to go back on duty. Before he left, however, I found that the whole of the field force were employed in a cross-pattern search well to the north of us. They had found no tracks as yet, and there were no reinforcements expected for some time. Then I went with the old man back to the farm.

I sat in his living-room trying to find the words to tell him, when suddenly he asked, 'What time are you leaving?'

I looked up. 'Just now. How did you know?'

He smiled. 'That savage of yours has been padding around all afternoon, like a lion that's smelled blood.'

The old man limped painfully across to the gun cabinet, unlocked it and took out a rifle. He balanced it lovingly across his arm. Then he held it out to me.

'Take it,' he said. 'It's old but it'll never let you down.'

It was a beautiful rifle with patterns worked into the barrel, and the stock was carved and polished by hand.

'Go on, take it,' he said. 'It'll help me feel as though I am with you.'

He handed me the rifle. I checked to make sure that it was empty, then I glanced down the sights and worked the oiled mechanism. The old man nodded approvingly.

'They don't make them like that any more,' he said.

He took a Browning repeating shotgun from the cabinet. 'This is for Katchemu,' he said, 'and here are plenty of heavy-bore cartridges for it. It'll suit that savage of yours. A blast from one of these at close range will blow a man in half.'

'Will you do me a favour?' the old man asked suddenly.

'What is it?'

'Take Dizarki and his son with you.'

I shook my head. 'The two of us are enough. He's an old man, he'd get in the way. Besides I thought that you and he had sent his eldest son to university. Has he come back?'

'Yes, in a manner of speaking. But it's not his eldest son he's taking with him. It's his second son. And as for getting in the way,' the old man's eyes flashed, 'Dizarki was hunting with me before you were born. Man, he's worth three of you in the bush and you need all the help you can get.'

'All right,' I said, 'I'll take him. Where is he?'

'Waiting downstairs with your boy.'

'Have they got rifles?'

The old man nodded. 'His son's got a Greener shotgun, and I told Katchemu to give Dizarki Andrew's .303.'

Katchemu, Dizarki and his son, Philemon, were waiting silently for me at the bottom of the stairs. I tossed Katchemu the Browning and two bags of cartridges. Katchemu was delighted. He ran his fingers lovingly over the polished barrel.

'One terrorist, two terrorists,' he chanted softly as he slipped five cartridges into the chamber.

I looked round them. 'There is a white one,' I said softly. 'You will leave that one for me.' They nodded.

'Have you fired one of these,' I asked.

'Many times on the range,' Katchemu answered. 'This gun is too wonderful. Tell me,' he asked, 'is it true that it can blow a man in half?'

'Yes,' I answered shortly.

He clutched the rifle tightly as though frightened that someone might steal it.

We changed in the garage and buried our clothes. I rubbed mud and oil into my face and hands to darken them, and fitted a long-bladed hunting knife, which the old man had given me, onto my belt. Then we set off across the vlei below the house, towards the Devil's Playground.

Something made me turn. I looked up and saw the old man watching us from the stoep. He waved, then his voice came floating down across the empty bush towards me.

'Good hunting,' he called.

CHAPTER FIFTEEN

RUNNING . . . Running easily in long loping strides in the pale half-light of the moon, my rifle held ready across my chest, the others following in single file, our muffled footsteps thudding on the sand.

I glanced at my watch. It was nearing ten o'clock. I wanted to be in the rocks – seven miles away – by eleven. The ceremony would be in full swing by then.

The narrow path wound through clumps of stunted trees and small kopjes. Occasionally a nightjar, resting black upon the still warm sand, would start almost under my feet, its wings brushing up against my legs, while red eyes from the bush followed our passing and called warnings down the line.

After three-quarters of an hour the first stark shapes of the balancing rocks came into sight, twisted and grey in the moonlight. I raised my hand above my head to signal a halt and then squatted in the shadow of a rock. The others joined me. We were all panting from exertion, but I noticed that Dizarki had many miles left in him. I touched Philemon's shoulder. 'Keep watch,' I whispered and he moved silently up the path.

I looked at my watch. It was ten minutes to eleven.

'Farther on,' I said softly, 'we will come to a place where the path forks. Dizarki, you and your son will take the right fork. You know the place where the Madam used to play when she was young. It is within this circle that the people are. Climb to the top so that you can see them. Then wait until you hear my first shot. You will not fire until you hear my shot. Do you understand?'

'I hear you, Mambo,' Dizarki said softly.

I glanced up. The shadows obliterated the outline of his face. But his eyes glinted cruelly in the dark, and I was glad that the old man had sent him.

We checked our rifles, waiting for our breathing to slow. Then we set off again on the final stretch.

A ground mist had formed at the foot of the rocks. It swirled around our thighs, muffling our footsteps, leaving only the dark silhouette of each man and his rifle from the waist up, seemingly floating on its surface.

At the fork Dizarki stopped. He looked as though he was about to say something, a half-formed word on his lips. Then he changed his mind.

'Watch out for guards,' I whispered as he disappeared into the shadows.

We moved slowly forward for another two hundred yards feeling our way along the path. Then Katchemu tapped me lightly on the shoulder. I spun round raising my rifle. He touched his ear then he pointed in the direction of the arena. I stood listening for a moment and I caught the faint eerie sounds of drumming, muffled by the mist. If I ever got back alive, I promised, I would give the mad woman the biggest lighter that I could find.

We reached the elephant grass. I pulled Katchemu down beside me. Before us lay the tunnel.

'There'll be a guard,' I whispered. He nodded and we both moved off in different directions to find him. The drumming was louder now and the red glare from the fire inside the arena reflected off the walls and up against the low white clouds, tingeing them scarlet.

I slung the rifle over my shoulder and moved silently through the grass, the knife in my hand, pausing every few steps to listen. A few minutes later Katchemu whistled softly. Then he crawled up beside me.

'One on the other side of the tunnel,' I whispered. 'The light flashes through every time he moves.'

'One more up there,' Katchemu pointed. I glanced upwards through the grass. A guard was crouching on the wall looking very much like another rock, except for the rifle cradled in his arms, the barrel of which he had forgotten to darken and which was glinting in the moonlight. 'He's just moved round from the other side,' Katchemu whispered.

'He's going to be bloody hard to get.'

'I know a way,' Katchemu answered softly, 'a very good way. Move directly under him, Mambo, and wait until the moon passes behind a cloud. Then scratch on the rock with a stone. Scratch hard because of the drums.' Katchemu drew a long thin knife from his waist and balanced the copper-bound handle in his hand. 'By the time he sees you he'll be dead,' he whispered softly.

I crawled silently through the grass towards the wall. A few minutes' search and I found a small sharp flint. Then I sat below the guard with my back against the rock, watching through a parting in the grass for a cloud to darken the moon.

The guard stirred to a more comfortable position. His rifle chinked against a rock. A cloud bank was moving towards the moon now. I began to count ... nine ... eight ... seven. I was counting the seconds of the man's life away. I grasped the stone and turned to the rock. Five ... four. The cloud darkened the rim of the moon. Black shadows ran across the elephant grass towards the wall. When they were almost on me, I started to scratch at the rock like an antbear sharpening his claws. I heard the guard lean over the edge, peering down into the grass below him.

'Now, Katchemu, now,' I breathed. 'In a moment the cloud will have passed.'

There came a dull whirr as the twisting knife sped over my head. Then a sickening thud as it struck home. I started up. The guard half-stood, half-crouched, his mouth wide open in a wordless scream, his hands tearing at the long slender hilt of the knife lodged in his stomach. He dropped his rifle. Then slowly, very slowly, he toppled forward off the wall.

Katchemu appeared beside me and together we broke his fall and dropped him softly on the ground. With a savage grunt Katchemu pulled out his knife and cut the guard's throat to make sure. Then he wiped it clean on the dead man's shoulder.

I looked up. The cloud was some way past the moon. Katchemu grinned at me.

'Mambo,' he whispered, 'the first blood of the hunting.'

We wedged the dead man in the tunnel. Soon the first stages of rigor mortis would set in and the stiffened corpse would effectively block the entrance. Then we started up the wall using the natural faults in the rock as foot-holes.

The top was nearly flat and ten foot wide in places. We crawled across to the edge and, from the cover of some boulders, looked down into the arena. Below us some thirty Africans were gathered, squatting in neat rows. A blazing fire separated them from the altar stone, and facing them, before the altar stone, was a man dressed in white flowing robes. On his left was another man similarly dressed but in black. On his right was a third dressed in red, holding a lantern. Four others moved on the fringes of the crowd with sub-machine-guns slung over their shoulders.

The man in white stepped forward. He was only about five feet tall. The firelight shone in his face. It was chalk-white, with thick negroid lips and nose. Vivid running sores, where the sun had cracked his tender flesh, scarred his sunken cheeks and his chin. His head was covered by a cowl but it seemed as though his wide staring eyes had no lids, only half-circles of red running sores.

He lifted his arms and, at the signal, a drum started a slow deep beat like a metronome. The crowd swayed to its time.

'Whose spirit am I?' the albino screamed.

'Lobengula,' roared the crowd.

'That man is evil,' Katchemu said softly. 'He has the face of one who has been dead for a long time, but who was never buried. Perhaps he is a spirit.'

The albino darted forward and seemed to reach into the fire. The drum beat a fraction faster and the people swayed in rippling lines as though hypnotized, the sweat glistening on their backs from the previous dancing.

'Whose spirit am I?' the albino screamed. He held his arms outstretched, flames licking down from his shoulders to his hands, until he formed part of a blazing cross.

The acolytes started the chant and the crowd took it up. 'Lobengula – Lobengula – Lobengula – Lobengula – Lobengula.' The drum beat harder and the people's voices swelled.

Another signal. The drum stopped and with it the people.

'What am I called?' the albino screamed.

The drum started. 'Whispering Death,' the people chanted. 'Whispering Death.'

'Why?'

'Because none will hear you coming. Because none will hear you coming.'

'Who do you hate?'

'The Europeans. The Europeans. The Europeans.'

'Who will you follow?'

'The Whispering Death. The Whispering Death. The Whispering Death.'

The drum beat faster.

'Who will you kill?'

'The women and children. The women and children,' the crowd screamed.

The two acolytes stepped forward and smothered the flames on the albino's arms with blankets. He reached behind the altar stone and drew out a pole. There were long tresses of brown hair, matted with blood, fastened to its top.

'Like this,' he screamed. 'Like this.'

One of the acolytes took the pole and walked through the crowd. The people leaped up to touch the hair.

The albino took a handful of powder from a bag and threw it into the fire. Blue flames mingled with the red.

'Kill,' he screamed. 'Kill.'

'Kill,' the people answered. 'Kill.'

The albino threw another handful of powder onto the fire. It exploded into green flames.

'Kill,' he screamed. 'Kill.'

He threw on more powder until the fire burned with the colours of a rainbow. Other drums started to throb. The noise resounded against the walls until it was deafening.

'Kill,' the people screamed. 'Kill, kill, kill, kill.'

Someone started to dance. Others joined in. 'Kill, kill, kill.' The words shattered the air. A man danced into the fire and came out, his hair and clothes ablaze, screaming with ecstasy and pain. Another threw himself down at the feet of the albino and tried to kiss the hem of his dirty white robe.

The drums took on a faster beat. I heard a groan and spun round. Katchemu, his face bathed in sweat, was kneeling on the edge, swaying in time to the rhythm. Another moment and he would have leapt into the arena and joined them. I reached out for a rock and brought it smashing down on his head. Then I caught him by the scruff of his shirt and dragged him back.

For a moment he lay still, a thin trickle of blood running down his neck. Then he opened his eyes. I sighed with relief. I might have known that it would take more than a rock to crack his thick skull.

'Mambo,' he said softly. 'I'm sorry. It was the drums.'

We crawled behind the cover of the boulders. Dizarki and his son should be in position by now, but there was no way of knowing until the first shot was fired. I nodded to Katchemu. It was time to begin. He took up position on my left and we laid out our cartridges beside us for easy loading. In a few minutes I hoped, the hunt would be over.

A single drum was beating. The albino held the pole above his head. Then he dipped it slowly into the fire, and I saw Sally's hair burn.

'Now,' he screamed. 'The Oath.'

I sighted my rifle. A man could take as much as twenty minutes to die from a well-placed bullet in his lower stomach. 'Little man,' I breathed, 'now you die ... slowly.'

Suddenly a crack rang out from the other side of the arena, the blast echoing over the sound of the drum. The acolyte in black spun round clutching his shoulder. A second shot took him in the stomach and sent him sprawling on the ground. The drum stopped and a paralysed silence settled over the arena. In an instant the acolyte was up on his feet, staggering for cover. The third shot caught him full in the kidneys and he screamed, his legs weakening until he rested on his knees, his hands clutching his stomach, trying to hold back the blood. He remained on his knees for a moment, as though praying. Then he rolled over onto the sand, dead.

I loosed off a shot at the albino, but he had dodged behind the altar stone and my bullet wasted itself in the sand where he had stood.

Katchemu started firing. The blast from his shotgun nearly deafened me, while his spent cartridges fell lightly on my shoulders.

The cross-fire from our rifles was taking a terrible toll. The crowd panicked, each one desperately trying to find cover. If a man fell, they trampled him under, while bullets that went wide screamed off the walls and mingled with the cries of dying men. Then, in desperation, they charged us.

I picked out a man with a spear held ready to throw, and waited until he was some twenty yards away. Then I shot him through the head. He sprang high into the air. Then his legs crumpled under him as he landed and he fell twitching to the ground.

Katchemu fired in bursts of five, singing out loud as the heavy shot spread out and cut men down. The attack faltered behind the dead bodies of its leaders. Then the remainder turned and ran.

Suddenly, from behind the altar stone, there came the first harsh, hesitant stammer of a sub-machine-gun. Its bullets screamed over our heads. Two others joined in and the darkened altar stone was lit by their scarlet flashes.

The light from a powerful hunting-torch probed for us among the covering rocks. In a moment we would be pinned down. At close range like this our rifles were no match for machine guns. I knelt up firing wildly at the light.

'Jump, Katchemu,' I shouted. 'Roll as you hit the ground so you don't break your ankles.' But Katchemu didn't move.

'Mambo, the killing's only just started,' he answered obstinately.

The white beam of light silhouetted my head against the sky, and I threw myself down spreadeagled behind the boulder. Bullets whined in amongst the rocks searching like steel fingers for my body.

We were safe where we lay. But now that they had pinned us down they could take their time to unblock the tunnel and outflank us. Once they did that, we were dead.

Katchemu was laughing to himself. I looked across angrily. 'Mambo,' he chuckled, 'did you see how that spirit ran when he thought that he was going to get shot?'

I borrowed his Browning and edged forward. One quick blast at the light was all I needed. The spacing of the shot would take care of the rest. As soon as the barrel showed above the boulder it was met by a hail of bullets and I sank back.

'Oh God,' I thought. 'We were so close. If I live I'll probably never get that close again.'

The arena was silent now apart from the cries of the wounded and dying.

Suddenly I spotted a figure crawling around the edge of the wall behind the altar. A shot rang out. A man screamed and the light fell to the ground. I leaped up and blasted at it. The light went out as the heavy lead pellets tore the torch to shreds. The terrorists turned their attention on the man behind them. I could see the sparks flying up as their bullets ricocheted off the rock. There was no answering fire.

'Time to get out of here,' I whispered. Katchemu did not answer. I punched him on the shoulder. 'Come on,' I ordered tossing him back the Browning. He followed me unwillingly and covered me as I climbed down the wall. One quick glance in the tunnel told me that they had not yet succeeded in removing the body. Then I covered Katchemu's descent.

'Mambo,' he breathed as he joined me, 'did you ever see such fighting? Did you ever hear of such a killing?' He shook his head delightedly. 'The tale of this night will be told even unto our great-great-grandchildren. And this gun,' he held it up in the moonlight, 'was there ever such a wonderful gun, Mambo? One big bang, and so many men are dead.'

'What about the albino?' I asked icily. 'He got away, remember.'

Katchemu shrugged his huge shoulders. 'Now, Mambo,' he said happily, 'we can really hunt him. And he will die little by little over the days.'

'Just you shut up,' I said furiously, and led the way back in silence to the rock from which we had first started.

We waited for half an hour. Katchemu suddenly signalled to me. Then Dizarki materialized from the mist like a shadow.

I swung up my rifle and pointed it at his chest. 'You bastard,' I whispered, nearly crying with rage, 'tell me one reason why I shouldn't shoot you. The albino was only half a second from dying. What was the man in black to you that you should spoil everything?'

'He was my son,' Dizarki said slowly. 'The first-born.'

'How did you know?'

'I caught his wife carrying food from my kraal and I questioned her.'

He reached out and pushed the rifle barrel away from him. 'I thought only one shot and he would be dead,' he said sadly. 'Then you could kill the albino. But my hands trembled too much. Perhaps it was good that way.' He added, 'The Madam Sally was like my child.'

'Did the old man know when he sent you?' I asked.

Dizarki nodded. 'I told him before the funeral. He is wise, the old one, my Mambo. He knew that only the father can kill his first-born son with justice and bear the pain.' Dizarki looked up into my face and his eyes narrowed. 'If you had killed him, Mambo,' he said quietly, 'maybe I would have killed you, and that would make the old one sad.'

'And maybe I would have killed you,' Katchemu growled. Dizarki stiffened as he felt Katchemu's knife in his back.

I shook my head confused. 'From the time you spoiled my aim I hated you like I hate the albino. I don't know what to think now. I can't feel anything any more, only hate.'

Dizarki nodded. 'When you let hate fill your belly,' he warned, 'it runs up through your blood until you see only red till you die.'

'Where's Philemon?' Katchemu asked suddenly.

'They were lucky,' Dizarki said slowly. 'Their bullets caught him in the throat when he shot the man with the light.'

'What will you do now?' I asked.

'When the dawn comes I will bury my son. Then I will go back to my Mambo. It is good that we should be together in times like this.'

'We'll bury your first-born son for you,' I said.

'No,' Dizarki said fiercely. 'Leave him for the vultures like the rest. I had only one son.'

'Katchemu, let him go,' I said softly.

He walked off into the bush. 'You're lucky that you have hate.' His voice came from the dark, 'I am old, I only have pain now.' Then he was gone.

In the shelter of a small cave a mile away from the arena I ⎵ped my rifle and haversack and fell exhausted to the ground. Ten minutes later Katchemu appeared. 'There is no one following,' he murmured.

'How much longer to dawn?' I asked.

Katchemu glanced up at the sky. 'Maybe in four hours. I'll take the first watch of two hours. I'll wake you for your turn.' He sat as still as a rock at the entrance of the cave with his shotgun across his knees, the barrel dulled with mud to prevent it glinting in the waning moonlight.

I scratched a shallow hole in the ground for my hips and lay back using my haversack as a pillow. For a while I stared into the darkness, thinking of Dizarki. I remembered him as he stood by the rock with Katchemu's knife in his back, too proud and fierce to show the agony in his soul; only the voice from the dark that pleaded for understanding, and I, nearly crying with rage, too filled with hate to understand the sacrifice he had made. Suddenly I felt tears running down my cheeks. 'Oh, Dizarki,' I said softly into the dark, 'I'm sorry.'

Katchemu turned at the sound of my voice. 'Mambo, are you dreaming?' he asked. I did not answer. He crept down the cave and crouched over me. He must have seen the tears for he shook his head. 'Sleep Mambo,' he said softly, 'sleep now.'

I thought of Sally, her dark fathomless eyes looking up into mine, her arms circled around my neck. 'Darling, it doesn't matter what happens so long as I'm with you. You see I love you. I love you so very much. Goodbye little cottage. See you on Saturday after we're married.'

'I love Sally, I love Sally and I always will.'

'Put me down.'

'In fact I love the whole world. I love you. I love the sun. I love the air and the land. I love just being young and being about to be married to the most beautiful girl in the world.'

The flames licking up through the thatched roof of the cottage ... Sally lying naked on the sand, red gashes where their knives had torn into her, two streaks of dried tears running down her cheeks ... the albino lowering the pole and her hair burning in the fire.

Dizarki's voice came warning me from the dark. 'When

you let hate fill your belly it runs up through your blood until you see only red till you die.'

I rolled over onto my stomach. Suddenly I was shivering so hard that I had to bite my hand to stop my teeth from chattering. Then my tired brain refused to function any more and I drifted gratefully into sleep.

CHAPTER SIXTEEN

'WHAT do you want?' the old man asked.

Peter shuffled awkwardly in his chair. 'I came to find out how you were.'

'Not at one o'clock in the morning you didn't,' the old man said coldly.

'Well then, where's Terick?'

The old man shrugged his shoulders, 'I don't know.'

'Where's Katchemu then?'

'I don't know.'

'Where's Dizarki?'

The old man shook his head. 'I don't know.'

'Yes you bloody well do,' Peter said angrily. 'Where are they?'

'What do you want to know for? So that you can go and tell Bill?'

'No,' Peter said furiously half-rising from his chair. 'Now look, you bloody old man. I'm his best friend and I was going to be best man at his wedding. I've got a right to know where he is.'

'Now you listen you ... you young skelm. He didn't tell me where he was going and I didn't ask him. It was better that way. Besides if you are his best friend why aren't you with him?'

'Because I can't find him – bugger it,' Peter said, miserably sinking back in his chair.

The Member in Charge was asleep, hunched up in the front seat of a Land Rover, his head resting uncomfortably against the window-pane. Ian opened the door and tapped him on the shoulder. 'They're here,' he said briefly.

The Member in Charge climbed stiffly out of the driver's seat and walked towards the camp fire where the Chief of the Reserve and the mad woman were waiting for him. His eyes were red with weariness and the stubble of a beard lined his cheeks.

'This is the lighter, Bill,' Ian said handing it over to him. The Member in Charge held it in front of the mad woman.

'Where did you get this from?' he asked. The initials 'TH' were engraved on the side. The mad woman didn't answer.

'This one is too difficult, Mambo,' a constable at her side volunteered. The Member in Charge nodded. He was used to dealing with difficult people.

'You stole this, didn't you?' he said softly, juggling the lighter in his hand.

The mad woman shook her head.

'It belonged to a white man. See,' the Member in Charge showed her the initials on the side. 'You stole it,' the Member in Charge said again softly, 'and for this you will go to jail.'

The mad woman shook her head violently.

'You will go to jail and live in a cell until you die,' the Member in Charge said firmly.

'The white man gave it to me,' the mad woman said sullenly.

'Why?' the Member in Charge asked.

'Because I told him about the young men going to the meeting in the rocks.'

'When was this?'

'Yesterday, in the afternoon.'

'When was the meeting?'

'Last night.'

'Where?'

'I only know in the haunted rocks.'

'Where?' the Member in Charge asked again.

The mad woman shook her head. 'I only know in the rocks,' she repeated.

The Member in Charge glanced into her face and satisfied himself that she was telling the truth. 'She can go,' he said to the constable standing above her. The mad woman rose and held out her hand.

'It's mine,' she said pointing to the lighter. The Member in Charge gave it back to her. She flicked it a few times but the gas had run out and she threw it into the fire. Then she muttered something over her shoulder as she walked away.

'She says why don't you arrest him,' the indignant constable interpreted, 'because he cheated her.'

'Tell her if she's not out of this camp in three minutes,' the Member in Charge bellowed, 'by God I'll find some way to put her in jail.'

He turned to the Chief of the Reserve. 'Now you,' he said. The Chief shifted uncomfortably before the fire. 'You knew there was this meeting.' The Chief saw no point in lying and he nodded. 'And you knew that some of your young men were going.' The Chief nodded again. He was an elderly man with a battered white pith-helmet about his ears and a chain around his neck linking a design in the centre which denoted his rank.

For a moment the Member in Charge stared at the Chief in silence. The Chief shifted uncomfortably under his accusing gaze.

'Big Mambo,' he said softly, 'my people are peaceful. You know that. We never cause troubles. All we care for is our land and our crops and our cattle. The Native Commissioner comes to us and tells us to do stupid things, like put strange powder on the land before we plant our crops, or make our cattle swim through strong waters. And we do it because we do not want troubles.

'Now these men come from the rocks. And they speak to ⟨o⟩f fighting and killing until we are very much afraid. They tell us that they will take over this land, killing all the Europeans. They say to my young men that they can have these Europeans' farms if they follow them. And there is one, the spirit of the Chief Lobengula, of whom we are very much afraid. He says that he has come to lead us. And if we do not follow him he will kill us. Now Mambo,' the Chief looked up, 'what am I to do? For these men are very strong and fierce. If they take this land you will go to the South, or to your home across the seas. But what of me, Mambo, and my people? Where can we run? No, we must stay and if they learn that we have helped you, they will kill us.'

In his heart the Member in Charge had to admit the logic of the Chief's argument. He pointed to the grey menacing shapes of the Land Rovers parked in lines at the edge of the camp, and then to the men as they slept by their fires, their rifles ready beside them.

'We are stronger,' he said softly. 'We will not run. We have no other home but this one. You were wrong not to trust us.'

'Can I trust you at three o'clock in the morning when a man comes to my kia with a knife?' the Chief asked.

'You can trust me,' the Member in Charge bluffed, 'because behind that man there will be one of my constables with a gun pointing at his back.'

The Chief smiled unbelievingly. 'I will help you,' he said at last, 'because, if I don't, you will tell the Native Commissioner and he will take away my Chieftainship. And I have grown accustomed to this chain about my neck.'

The Member in Charge stood up and the Chief rose with him. 'All the years,' the Member in Charge promised, 'as long as you live in peace and within the law you can watch your children grow and your cattle fatten on the rich grass without fear, for I will protect you.'

'That, Mambo,' the chief said sincerely, 'is what I hope.'

The Member in Charge watched the Chief walk slowly out of sight, escorted by his messengers. Then he turned to Ian. 'Get your men ready,' he said. 'We'll start searching those rocks at first light.'

CHAPTER SEVENTEEN

As the first red tinges of dawn showed against the clouds and mingled with the cold grey of the rocks we huddled over a tiny fire, made by pouring small quantities of paraffin into loose sand, and sipped steaming mugs of thick curried soup. Then, as the rim of the sun showed above the eastern horizon, we moved back to the arena, for the human eye can track a spoor best in the early morning or the late afternoon. Then the shadows accentuate the faintest impressions on the earth by giving them a depth and width that could not otherwise be seen.

Vultures had already begun to gather on the walls and a smell of death hung over the place. The terrorist had been removed from the tunnel and laid on one side, the ants swarming on the wounds in his neck and his stomach.

We waited for a further ten minutes until the sun was almost clear of the horizon and the ground mist began to fade. Then Katchemu grunted. 'The light is all right now.'

He followed the trail through the grass and some two hundred yards on into the rocks, until it was clear of our tracks from the previous night. He then began to cast around, running forward a little way and retracing his steps, his hands feeling the marks and measuring the distances between the prints. I followed some ten yards behind to guard against an ambush.

Something was puzzling him. He began to whisper, cursing himself when he missed a clue and congratulating himself when he found it. 'Follow, Katchemu,' he kept urging himself. 'Follow like a dog on the scent of a bitch.' Suddenly he dodged into the bush and returned with a bamboo pole. placed the pole between two sets of footprints and cut notches in it to measure the distance. Then he set off back along the track, stopping every few paces to measure again.

'Mambo,' he called at last, and I walked over. 'There are four men walking and two of them are carrying a man. He must be tied between two poles, for see these prints.' He pointed them out with the stick, 'and these, and these.' He moved farther down the line. 'They are always deeper than the rest, and the same distance apart. And they always walk with the same foot first. The other two are carrying the extra packs for, look, the big toe is deeper in the earth from balancing the weight.'

All I could see were faint smears in the rock-hard earth. 'How do you know it's a man they are carrying?' I asked dubiously.

'Must be a man,' Katchemu replied indignantly. 'The poles are eight foot apart.'

'All right then, let's go,' I said impatiently. Every moment that we wasted increased the terrorists' lead. Katchemu squatted on the ground.

'No hurry, Mambo,' he said calmly. 'They will soon be tired with all the weight they are carrying. Then they won't watch so hard and we'll catch them easy.'

He studied each footprint. By its size he could form a good estimate of the man's height and weight. Then he memorized the way the toes were twisted or the distance of the instep until he could recognize each man even though his tracks were joined by others.

The sun burned down from a cloudless sky as we marched. The shimmering rays of heat made the rocks dance in the distance. The sweat poured down my face and chest, darkening my shirt with its sticky, cloying dampness. I kept rubbing my hands on my trousers, afraid that in an emergency they might slip when they gripped my rifle. My pack grew heavier with each stride.

At about one o'clock Katchemu stopped in the shade of a kopje.

'Mambo,' he called excitedly, 'tney rested here. Look, they put the man down. I was right when I told you.'

I nodded. In the dust I could see the imprint of two poles lying side by side some three feet apart.

Katchemu kicked at the marks. 'This one must be important for them to have carried him so far.'

'Could it be the albino?' I asked hopefully.

Katchemu shook his head. 'Too heavy,' he replied.

Clouds of flies were swarming around us and I wearily brushed them off. Katchemu watched them and his eyes narrowed.

'There is something here,' he said. He sniffed at the hot still air. Then he set off into the bush. I found him on his knees scooping away the earth near an anthill. After a few seconds he sat back and drew out a wad of blood-soaked bandages. Beneath it was a pile of human dung.

'I told you they were getting tired,' he said delightedly. 'They didn't dig it deep enough.' He examined the state of the dried blood. 'This one will die soon,' he announced. Then he turned his attention to the dung. He unlaced his boot and buried his toes in it, feeling its warmth. 'Maybe two hours in front,' he said. 'That's all.'

He wiped his foot clean on the grass and re-covered the hole. Then he glanced at my face. 'We'll rest for twenty minutes,' he said.

'Ten,' I cut in, angry that he had seen me tired.

'Ten minutes.' He shrugged his shoulders and moved back to the shade of the kopje.

I sat gratefully on a stone beside him and loosened my pack. Then I felt in my pockets for a cigarette and offered him one. He shook his head.

'In the bush, Mambo, a trained man can smell smoke two hundred yards away. At night the tip of a cigarette can be seen at half a mile. A whisper travels half as much again during the dark as it does during the day. These are dangerous things that you must know when you are hunting men, for they in turn may hunt you.'

I took the cigarettes a little way into the bush and buried them. When I returned he nodded approvingly.

'You are learning,' he said.

I took a sip from my water-bottle and shrugged on my pack. Katchemu handed me a small round knot of white wood which he had cut from a nearby tree.

'Suck this,' he said. 'It'll help the thirst.'

'If we get ahead of them now we might be able to ambush them. It should be easy if they are as tired as you say they are.'

Katchemu shook his head. 'We'll stay one hour behind them, Mambo, until nearly sunset. Then we'll move up to half an hour. The time after the sun has set, and before the moon rises, is the time to attack. During these minutes you can stalk within five yards of a man and he cannot see you, for his eyes have not yet grown accustomed to the dark and there are no shadows. Remember, Mambo, if you hunt a man at this time and he turns, stay still, do not move. Though you are almost on him, if you stay still, though you are ten yards in front of a tree, he will think that you are part of the trunk. He cannot tell distance until there is shadow from the moon or the sun.'

A dog can track a clean scent for miles across the bush if it is fairly fresh, but after a while he grows tired and his attention wanders to more interesting game. Then you find that you have to keep drawing him in to check that he is not following buck.

Katchemu could follow the same track for weeks and never grow tired. He could almost watch a blade of grass rising two hours after his quarry had brushed past it, showing me how the bruise, where the blade had been struck, shone against the dull green of the rest. When the earth gave way to stony ground he did not have to slow his pace for he could tell at a glance, by the scratches or where a stone had been turned, showing a rough face instead of a weathered one, the direction the terrorists had taken.

Three more hours went by. The heat was unbearable. Not

even a faint breeze stirred the grass. The barrels of our rifles and the buckles on our belts became too hot to touch. Sweat poured into my eyes and my mouth. My back where the pack rubbed against it became a mass of blisters, and the glare from the sun off the rocks hurt so much that I thought my brains were boiling.

I kept fingering my water-bottle, willing myself not to drink, while the little knot of wood rattled dryly in my mouth. Then I thought of the men in front. I pictured the albino's face through a haze of pain and sweat, the sun burning on his red-rimmed staring eyes set into the tender clammy whiteness of his skin, and the flies settling on his open sores. It would be worse for him, much worse, and the thought eased my pain.

As the sun began to dip Katchemu marched faster, until at last he held up his hand. I staggered to a halt below a slight rise. He pointed to the tracks. 'They are struggling,' he said. 'The weight is too much. If they wish to keep up this speed they will have to kill the wounded one tonight so that they can bury him out of sight.'

'What do we do now?' I asked.

'You wait,' he answered. 'They will have to stop very soon. Their feet won't carry them much farther. I will go forward and find their camp then come back for you.'

Katchemu returned silently. 'It was as I thought,' he said softly. 'They have camped twenty minutes farther on in some fever trees at the bottom of a kopje. They do not know that they are being followed because they are lighting a fire. There is a guard halfway up the kopje. We must kill him first.'

He stretched out beside me. 'Now we rest,' he said.

CHAPTER EIGHTEEN

THE Member in Charge stood on the bonnet of a Land Rover at the base camp in the foothills of the Devil's Playground. Behind him came the light from a dozen cooking fires, and assembled in a half-circle around him were a crowd of tired farmers, the dirt and sweat drying on their unshaven faces.

The Member in Charge cleared his throat and nervously fumbled for his pipe. 'At noon today,' he began, 'the bodies of seventeen terrorists and would-be terrorists were found in this area, together with two more wounded who are not expected to live.' The drawn faces of the farmers began to brighten. 'We had no patrols in the area,' the Member in Charge admitted, 'and it's been established that these men were killed in a night ambush by Terick and his boss boy, Katchemu. We think that there may have been others, but we've no evidence.' The Member in Charge stopped.

'He's done it,' the crowd said excitedly amongst themselves. 'Did you hear that? He's bloody done it.'

'Several of the terrorists,' the Member in Charge continued, 'are known to have escaped. They are heading deeper into the rocks, and we believe that Terick's following them. I immediately informed the OC of this development and I have received very definite instructions. Terick must be stopped at all costs. I have no need to point out to you that he has blatantly committed mass murder.'

For a moment the crowd were stunned. Then van Sittart, a huge Afrikaans farmer, called up, 'What are you telling us? Speak straight, man.' The crowd murmured their agreement.

'Van,' the Member in Charge said slowly, 'I'm trying to tell you that tonight, when we move into the rocks, the first thing that we're going to have to do is catch Terick before he can kill any more of them.'

'What happens to him then?' Van asked cautiously.

'He'll be tried for murder,' the Member in Charge replied.

'And what about the terrorists?'

'They're of secondary importance now. We'll catch them later. The main thing is to stop Terick.'

'You mean arrest him?' Van's understanding of English was never very good.

'Yes. Shoot him in the legs if you have to. You understand why, don't you?' the Member in Charge said almost pleadingly.

Van nodded. Then he exploded, his full grey beard quivering with rage. He turned to the crowd. 'Peoples,' he shouted. 'Peoples, you know me, Van. I'm nothing special and my English is not so good. But, peoples, listen. They say to me, "Van, come and hunt terrorists." I leave my wife and my children and my cattle, but I come. And all day I sweat in the bush because I think it's right. These men must be caught.

'Now they say to me, "Van, go and hunt Terick because he has killed these terrorists." Peoples, they kill his woman, they burn his farm, they kill his boys. But when he kills them he must be arrested. "Van," I say to myself, "is this right?" And, peoples, I ask you, say to yourself, "is this right?" '

'Look,' the Member in Charge shouted above the angry crowd, 'Rhodesia cannot afford to let a white man run around murdering Africans. World opinion is against us as it is. To them these aren't terrorists, they're freedom fighters. They're just looking for an excuse like this.'

'Bugger world opinion,' someone shouted. 'What does it mean anyway?'

'Don't keep calling it murder,' someone else shouted. 'It's plain justice – you know it is.'

'It's murder,' the Member in Charge shouted back. 'Terick was a policeman. He knows the law. He knows that revenge is no excuse for killing people.'

'Don't call them people, they're terrorists.'

'Look Bill,' someone shouted. 'We need to talk about this.'

Before the Member in Charge could stop them, the farmers went into a huddle some way from the Land Rover. When they returned Van had been elected their spokesman. They knew that his English was not very good, but they liked the way he expressed himself.

'The peoples have decided we're sorry, but bugger you,' Van said.

The Member in Charge's face hardened. 'I'm not asking you,' he said, 'I'm telling you. It's an order.'

Van stood astride, his rifle held like a toy across his chest. 'Bugger your orders,' he replied for the crowd. 'We can't go against you, 'cause you the law. But we're not going to help you, so we're going home.'

The Member in Charge wondered for a moment if he could threaten to arrest them. Then he decided against it. In the temper they were in, each farm would probably go into laager and he'd find himself with forty small wars on his hands.

The Member in Charge climbed down from the bonnet and watched the farmers collect their kit and slowly disappear, each taking with him his boys from the African Police Reserve until the camp was empty apart from a few regulars.

Ian walked up and stood beside him. 'You did your best, Bill,' he said sadly. 'Not even you can do the impossible.'

'Thanks,' the Member in Charge replied bitterly. 'Now I'd better go and inform the OC of that.' And he walked over to the Land Rover.

CHAPTER NINETEEN

THE last faint traces of crimson were fading in the western sky. 'It's time,' Katchemu grunted, rising to his feet.

We hid our packs, taking with us only our rifles and our

knives. Then we moved silently through the bush in a half-circle that would lead us out on the other side of the kopje above the guard.

I followed Katchemu up the kopje, using his hand and foot holes. It was amazing that a man of his bulk could move so silently. Instinct seemed to warn him which stone would bear his weight and which would roll. Below the ridge he paused and I drew myself up beside him. It was important that our breathing was controlled before we moved in.

I glanced anxiously up at the sky. In about ten minutes the moon would rise, lighting the land like a hazy day.

Katchemu grinned at me. We were breathing normally now. I tapped my knife. I would do it. He nodded. Then he touched my shoulder for luck. I started over the ridge of the kopje with Katchemu covering my back.

Way below me I could see the light from the camp fire in the fever trees, and the soft voices from the men around it rose on the still night air. By Katchemu's directions the guard would be a hundred yards down and slightly to the right.

I started to move towards him, flitting from cover to cover, wary of loose stones beneath my feet. Katchemu followed me at a distance. When I was twenty yards away from the spot where the guard should be I dropped to my knees and drew my knife, making sure that the blade was dulled with mud. Then I took off my shirt, pulling the sleeves inside out, and did the top button up over my head, cutting two slits across the chest for eye-holes. If the guard should turn the shirt would break the outline of my head and shoulders.

I glanced up. Only five minutes left. Already the sky was divided into shades of blue. I crawled on for another twelve yards and spotted the sentry. He was sitting on a rock with his back to me, overlooking the camp. The kopje sloped gently down towards him. There remained eight yards open ground with not even a small boulder for cover.

I edged towards him on my belly. Fifteen feet, twelve, ten. A stone, dislodged by my boot, rolled noisily past me and on towards the guard. He spun round, his rifle rising in line with his eyes. A cold sweat began to prickle on my exposed back. I buried my face in the earth taking slow shallow breaths, trying hard to believe in Katchemu's advice. The sentry stood up and I heard him start to walk towards me. Common sense screamed in me to run for cover. Anything was better than lying here waiting for a shot in the back. But I remained frozen like a dark patch of earth.

Suddenly another stone came rolling down from farther up the kopje, accompanied by a soft whine. The sentry picked up the stone and threw it over my head. It was answered by a sharp yelp, a sudden rustle and then silence.

'What's that?' a high piping voice called up from below.

'Wild dog,' the sentry called back softly.

I silently blessed Katchemu.

The man below grunted and the guard settled down on the rock again.

I counted slowly up to fifty. Then I began to edge forward again. 'I wonder if you have a god,' I spoke to the sentry in my thoughts. 'I wonder if you'll call on him as you die. Or perhaps you'll think of your woman, if you have one. Me! I'll think of Sally as I kill you.'

I rose silently behind him. Now. I snapped his head back with my left hand. For a split second I saw his eyes wide with terror and his teeth bit into my fingers. Then the knife slashed deep into his throat and his blood pulsed out across my hand and down onto his chest. I held him tightly for a moment as his body shuddered.

Katchemu appeared beside me. 'That was good,' he whispered. Then I laid him gently backwards on the ground. As his body relaxed, a small silvery object fell from his hand.

I went after it, to stop it, as it rolled down the kopje. 'Mambo,' Katchemu screamed after me, 'don't – it's a grenade.' The silvery object lodged between two small rocks in front of me.

I stopped dead. 'My God,' I just had time to think, 'he was sitting there with the pin out.' Then Katchemu grabbed my shoulders and threw me bodily behind a rock, his great bulk landing on top of me. The grenade went off with a deafening crack and the rocks around us were pitted by a rain of steel splinters. Then there was silence and swirling dust.

'Are you all right?' I asked breathlessly.

Katchemu nodded.

I started to my feet. 'Come on then. We can still take them by surprise.'

Katchemu reached out and pulled me roughly back behind the rocks.

'Too late,' he said fiercely. 'You know rifles are no good against them close up.' As he spoke a machine gun began to stammer below us, its bullets whining aimlessly in the rocks. 'At least up here they don't know where we are,' he said more gently. Then he looked at me for a moment. 'You know my Mambo,' he said softly, 'I thought you were dead then.' He rolled over and began to blast at the fever trees from the side of the rock.

I crawled twenty feet to another rock at right-angles to him and began to fire at the shadows in a five-yard circle around the fire. The moon was rising now and the high ground would give us the advantage.

After a few minutes the terrorists' fire slackened until only one gun occasionally sprayed the side of the kopje.

Katchemu crawled up beside me. 'They're leaving,' he said.

'Shall we follow?'

Katchemu shook his head. 'They can ambush us at night. Better to just follow when the light comes and strike again.'

'The one down there,' I nodded, 'must be the wounded one left to cover them.'

We moved slowly down the kopje, closing in on him. Suddenly his fire stopped in mid-burst. I knew the sound well. The highly complicated mechanism of his gun had jammed. There came frantic sounds as he tried to clear it.

I leapt to my feet and ran down the slope, my feet slipping on the loose rocks under me, my rifle held into my shoulder, the sights weaving in front of my eyes as I tried to fix on a target. Katchemu came after me, cursing as he strained to find footing. A shadow moved some thirty yards ahead and I fired as my sights came to bear. A baboon screamed and climbed to higher ground, clutching his arm like a human.

Suddenly I was on the flat ground and racing towards the camp, dodging and weaving as I ran. I leapt a small hillock. My feet slipped from under me and I found myself sliding down a bank into their camp. As soon as my feet hit solid ground I threw myself sideways, rolling over and over, my rifle clutched beneath me until I reached the cover of a rock. Then I spun up, my rifle sweeping in a wide arc encompassing the camp.

Katchemu came crashing down and rolled behind a small ant-hill. Automatically I swung my rifle up to give cover. But I was too late. A figure detached itself from the shadows and lunged at him. I caught the flash of a knife, a yell, then a ripping sound as it tore down to the bone. I dropped my rifle and threw myself at the terrorist dragging him off. We rolled over on the ground and I came up astride of him, wrenching the knife from his hand.

'Don't kill him,' Katchemu shouted. 'Don't kill him. He can talk.' The point of the knife was just piercing the skin of his throat. I stood up. The terrorist had fainted. I rolled him over and using the thongs from the poles, bound his hands behind his back.

I tore open Katchemu's shirt and looked at the wound. The blow had been deflected across his rib cage and on into the bone of his upper arm. There it had been twisted, leaving a gaping hole.

'Only stop the blood,' Katchemu said calmly. 'Otherwise it is nothing.'

I plugged it with rags and bound it tightly. Then I did the same for his chest.

'You need a hospital,' I said firmly, as I stood back.

Katchemu grinned. 'It is only a cut,' he said cheerfully. 'It getting stiff now, but by tomorrow it will be well again.'

I shook my head doubtfully.

'I've been cut before,' he reassured me. 'Many times. Now we must leave this place in case the others come back. Can you carry him?' he nodded to the terrorist.

'Yes.'

'Good, because there are many things that he is going to tell us,' Katchemu said grimly.

I walked across and picked up the machine gun. It was hopelessly jammed and I discarded it. Some half-open tins of food were spilt on the ground and empty cartridge cases were scattered here and there. Other than that there was nothing.

Katchemu looked up and saw my face. 'Don't worry, Mambo,' he said softly, 'I'll find them for you in the morning.'

CHAPTER TWENTY

THE Member in Charge picked up the telephone. When the operator answered he gave the number. 'It's a security call. Use the land line,' he added briefly.

The number rang once then a voice answered.

'The OC,' the Member in Charge said. He heard the sounds of footsteps hurrying across the room and the receiver was snatched up.

'Bill. Is that you?' came a harassed voice.

'Yes sir.'

'Thank Christ for that. I was afraid it might be the Minister again. He's phoned me twice already. I tell you this patrol officer of yours has sent PGHQ into a flat spin. They're taking it in turns to bollock me.'

The Member in Charge did not answer.

'So,' the voice came again more calmly, 'what happened?'

'They all went home, sir,' the Member in Charge said, resisting the impulse to add, 'as I warned you.'

'What!' the voice came aghast.

'They've all gone home,' the Member in Charge repeated.

'They can't do that. Arrest them for disobeying a lawful order or something.'

'With whom, sir?' the Member in Charge said bitterly.

The voice on the other end was silent for a moment. 'All right, Bill. I know you did your best. Look, there'll be a Captain Turnbull and a squad of SAS coming down. They should arrive before morning. Clear the landing area because there'll be a helicopter coming down with them. Bill,' the voice continued, 'Captain Turnbull will be taking charge of the operation when he arrives. I'll expect you to give him every assistance. You understand don't you?'

'Yes sir. You know, it's amazing.'

'What is?'

'Forty-eight hours ago they couldn't even spare a squad of Support Unit Askari. Now they're sending the bloody SAS and a helicopter. Has the overall situation changed that much?' the Member in Charge asked bitterly.

'You know it hasn't, Bill. But PGHQ and the Government are terrified of what the foreign Press will do to us over this. They'd send a squadron of Hunters down if it would help.'

'What are this Captain Turnbull's orders, sir?' the Member in Charge asked quietly.

'I don't know. He's being briefed at HQ but I should imagine he's been told to stop this bloke at all costs. Shoot him if he has to.'

'I thought it might be that,' the Member in Charge said.

'Well that's all then?'

'Yes, sir,' the Member in Charge replied.

'Well ... ah ... keep me informed,' the OC said awkwardly. Then he rang off.

CHAPTER TWENTY-ONE

I SAT on guard at the entrance to a small cave high up in the rocks. In the distance a jackal called to the rising moon and the wind moaned softly round me. Katchemu came up and squatted beside me.

'Is he conscious yet?' I asked.

Katchemu shook his head. 'That one should have died yesterday.'

'Did you try slapping his face?'

'Mambo,' Katchemu replied indignantly. 'I tried everything. If I hit him any harder I'd have killed him altogether.'

'So we wait,' I said wearily, and Katchemu nodded.

Below us the mist was rising, swirling like a grey sea through the rocks.

After a while we stole back into the cave. The terrorist lay still, eyes closed, pegged out with the thongs from his stretcher, like a star on the ground.

I shook my head. 'Not yet,' I said softly.

Katchemu suddenly jabbed his knife into the terrorist's thigh. His eyes flashed open with pain. 'So,' Katchemu warned, 'don't try to fool us again.'

I knelt beside the terrorist. 'Man,' I asked softly, almost in a whisper, 'do you speak English?'

The terrorist nodded. His face was grey from loss of blood and creased with pain.

'Then listen closely to me. First you tortured, then you killed my woman. You burnt my farm and you killed two of my boys. Now you will tell me where I can find your base camp. For I give you two choices. You can die quickly with little pain, or you can die screaming. But before you die,' I promised him, 'you will tell us.'

I sat back. 'Where is it?' I asked. The terrorist shook his head. 'Tell me.' He shook his head again. 'Tell me.' I commanded in a hoarse whisper, 'quickly.'

The terrorist began to shake his head from side to side. 'I cannot,' he screamed. 'I cannot. I cannot.'

'Tell me,' I shouted. 'Tell me.'

The terrorist began to cry in long aching sobs. Suddenly I lost control. I seized his neck and twisted his head from side to side, bumping it against the walls of the cave.

'You bastard,' I sobbed. 'Go on, you bastard, cry. She cried when you tortured her, didn't she? Didn't she? But you didn't stop. Did you? Did you? You didn't even know her yet you tortured her to death. And now you cry, you bastard.' My face was lined with tears. 'She never did you any harm. Neither did I. Neither did my boys. And yet you killed them and tortured her to death.' I sent his head crashing against the wall.

Katchemu pulled me off. 'Mambo,' he said quickly, 'it is better if I do it. This one will not live very long your way.'

I folded up against the wall of the cave. 'Why, Katchemu?' I asked. 'Why did they do that to her? Why did they hurt her so much?'

Katchemu put his hands on my shoulders to calm me. 'My Mambo,' he said gently. 'I don't know. People say that I am a savage because for me life is nothing but beer and women and fighting. And yet beside me this man is worse than the lowest animal.'

He turned and knelt beside the terrorist. His eyes seemed to glow in the dark of the cave as he cut away the blood-and-puss-soaked bandages that covered the terrorist's stomach, revealing an ugly festering wound.

'I am Katchemu,' he said softly. 'You will tell me, because I know ways that can even make the rocks to talk. Like if I light a slow fire of little balls of bush grass,' Katchemu nudged the wounded man. 'You hear that, animal?' he whispered. 'Little balls of bush grass burning on the wound in your stomach.'

'No,' the terrorist whispered, straining weakly at the thongs that held him fast. 'No you cannot. I am a soldier of the liberation army. You must treat me by the Geneva Convention as a prisoner-of-war.'

Katchemu looked puzzled. 'Geneva?' he asked. 'What is this?'

The terrorist raised his head. 'It means that you may not torture me. It is against the law. I must be taken to hospital for my wound and after it is healed, to jail.'

Katchemu laughed mirthlessly, pushing his head back. 'And my Madam?' he asked. 'Did you take her to hospital for her wounds?'

'I was ordered,' the terrorist whispered. 'I am a soldier. I was ordered.'

Katchemu prepared two compact balls of bush grass and sprinkled them with paraffin. Then he placed one of them on the terrorist's stomach, pressing it into the wound.

'Tell me,' he said.

The terrorist shook his head. Beads of sweat were running down his face.

'Are you so frightened of this great spirit who leads you?' Katchemu asked contemptuously. 'The one who runs from bullets and hides behind rocks. Soon, animal, you will be more frightened of Katchemu.'

He scraped a match against a rock. The bush grass flared up, lighting the whole cave for a brief second, then it burnt out leaving a stench of charred flesh. Again and again the terrorist's hoarse screams filled the air.

'The camp. Where is it?' Katchemu shouted above his wild gibbering. A second ball of bush grass flared up. The terrorist was dying fast.

He twisted his head to me, sobbing with pain. 'Have pity,' he whispered. 'Have pity.'

'When you burnt my farm and killed my woman I lost many things,' I snarled. 'And one of them was pity.' I nodded to Katchemu. He rolled a fresh ball and placed it on the terrorist's stomach.

'No,' the terrorist broke. 'No more. No more. No more.' He

closed his eyes tightly, inhaling the stench of his own charred flesh, and his body twitched with pain.

Katchemu held the lighted match over his face. 'Open your eyes, look at me and speak,' he ordered.

'Fifteen miles directly to the east from here,' the terrorist sobbed. 'A dry river bed. Follow it north for maybe twenty-five miles until you reach a pool. From there take the tallest kopje. On the west side three-quarters way up is a cave. It is there.'

'Now kill me,' he pleaded, 'for the pain is too terrible.'

'Who are the others?' Katchemu asked.

'There is the Spirit, the section leader and the commissar left. I was the radio operator.'

Katchemu glanced up at me. 'He's telling the truth,' he grunted. 'Is it all right?'

I nodded. He leant over and cut the terrorist's throat.

'That one was glad to die,' he said quietly. 'Do you feel better about the Madam now?'

I shook my head numbly. I was trembling so much that I could hardly sit still. 'I want the albino,' I choked and crawled out of the cave to be sick.

CHAPTER TWENTY-TWO

Ian walked into the Charge Office. 'Where's the Member in Charge?' he asked.

'In his office.'

'Alone?'

Sean nodded.

Ian knocked, then opened the door and walked in. The Member in Charge was sitting behind his desk with his feet on the window-ledge, a very tired man. He swung round as Ian entered.

'See the SAS are outside.'

The Member in Charge felt for his pipe. 'They've taken over,' he said briefly.

'I heard,' Ian said, finding a seat. 'What's this Captain Turnbull like?'

'Professional soldier. Good one I think.'

Ian smiled. 'I don't like your tone. Look Bill, it's probably better this way. You wouldn't have wanted to bring Terick in.'

'No,' the Member in Charge said slowly, lighting his pipe. 'I'm glad about that.'

'You see,' Ian smiled again, 'we professional soldiers have our uses. By the way,' he asked casually, 'where is Captain Turnbull?'

It was the Member in Charge's turn to smile. 'He's gone to question Johannes.'

'What?' Ian sat bolt upright in the chair with alarm. 'Why didn't you stop him?'

The Member in Charge shrugged his shoulders. 'I tried to warn him,' then he smiled, 'but you know what you professional soldiers are like.'

'My God,' Ian breathed, 'he's going to get a nasty surprise.'

And the Member in Charge agreed with him.

Half an hour later a Land Rover drew up outside the station. There came the sound of heavy boots on a wooden floor and Captain Turnbull burst into the office. He was a tall, fair, well-built man of about twenty-six, good-looking in a hard way. His face was white beneath his tan and his hands were still shaking.

'The old bugger,' he breathed, 'went for me with an elephant gun.'

Ian stood up and introduced himself.

'I'm telling you,' the Captain continued indignantly, 'he tried to kill me. The bullets were missing me by that much.' He indicated a fraction of an inch.

'Don't worry,' Ian said gently, trying to pacify him. 'He

must have just been warning you. The old man was a professional hunter. He wouldn't have missed.'

'Mind you,' the Member in Charge turned to Ian with a twinkle in his eye, 'he is getting old.'

'Why don't you arrest him?' the Captain demanded. 'He can't go around shooting at people like that.'

The Member in Charge shrugged his shoulders. 'You were on his land,' he said gently.

The Captain turned to Ian. 'Are they all like that around here?'

Ian nodded sympathetically. 'Most of them are just younger versions with newer rifles. I'd keep away from them if I were you.'

The Captain glanced at their faces and his expression hardened. 'Look,' he said, 'I've been sent down here to do a job. If I want information the people around here are bloody well going to tell me.'

'I know,' Ian said. 'But I'd do it tactfully if I were you.'

'Why should I?' The Captain glanced bitterly at the Member in Charge. 'I'm not a policeman, I'm a soldier. I'll do it my way.'

'You can bring in Terick and the terrorists,' the Member in Charge said, 'but you'll leave the people to me. I don't want you stirring them up any more. They're on the brink as it is. If you push them you'll find yourself with forty farmers and countless numbers of their boys in those rocks, all on Terick's side. Then we'll be in trouble.'

There came a knock on the door and an SAS sergeant entered. 'We're ready to move off, sir,' he announced to his captain.

'I'll be with you in a moment,' the Captain said shortly and the sergeant left the room.

'Will you withdraw your men from the area?' the Captain asked. 'They'll be in the way. I just need one with local knowledge.'

'Will I do?' the Member in Charge asked.

The Captain shook his head. 'I'm sorry,' he said, 'you're a bit too old and we move fast. Besides, I was hoping that you'd act as a liaison between me and HQ. I'll have to use runners because the terrorists will probably have a radio and can tune into our frequency. They've done it before.'

'How about Ian?' the Member in Charge asked. 'He's as old as me, but he was a full colonel and he knows what he's doing.'

The Captain looked at Ian with renewed respect. 'What regiment?' he asked.

'Gurkhas,' Ian replied.

The Captain shook his head regretfully. 'I'm sorry sir.'

'That's all right. I suppose you'd find it a bit embarrassing to have me looking over your shoulder all the time.'

'Oh it's not that, sir. It's like the Member in Charge. You're a bit too old. And besides,' the Captain said uncomfortably, 'the Army's changed a bit since your day. Couldn't I take that big bloke? I think his name's Peter. He seems to know what he's doing.'

'All right,' the Member in Charge said doubtfully. 'But I warn you, he is Terick's best friend. You might find yourself heading in the opposite direction. You'd better take the Sergeant Major as well.'

'OK,' the Captain said making for the door. 'Don't worry about this bloke Peter. I'll handle him. Is there anything else?'

The Member in Charge shook his head. 'I wouldn't be too sure about handling Peter,' he warned softly.

'By the way,' the Captain paused by the door. 'What's this bloke like? I mean, is he going to put up much of a fight?'

'It depends,' Ian said. 'If he's got the man he's after I think you'll be able to take him quite easily. But if you get in his way before he does, well then you'd better go carefully.'

'Don't worry,' the Captain said confidently. 'We'll have him back here in twelve hours. By the way, there are some Bushman trackers being flown down. Can you send them on to me when they arrive?'

'Watch out for Katchemu.' the Member in Charge called after him.

'Who's that?' the Captain poked his head round the door.

'His Boss boy.'

'Oh, I'd forgotten about him. Still I don't suppose he'll be any problem.'

The Member in Charge stared at the closed door.

'Fine troops, the SAS,' Ian said defensively. 'I mean, it's always the same in a crack regiment. The junior subalterns are frightened of their own footsteps, but when they get to be captains, and know what they're doing, they always get a bit cocky. Besides, it's true. We *are* too old to go chasing around the bush. We'd never keep up with them.'

'How do you know?' the Member in Charge asked indignantly. 'The Army's changed since your day.'

Ian winced. 'Well, it's probably true. He wasn't very tactful, that's all. But you've got to admit he's damned efficient.'

'I hope he comes face to face with Katchemu on a dark night,' the Member in Charge snorted. 'That'll reduce him to the cockiness of a corporal.'

The Captain walked into the Charge Office. 'Hey,' he said to Peter who was sitting on the counter talking to Sean, 'you're coming with me.'

Peter jumped lightly to the floor. 'All right,' he said, 'but man, I'm warning you, I'm coming for only one reason, and that's to make sure that you or your men don't shoot Terick. 'Cause man, if you do,' Peter warned, 'you're going to have an accident.'

'A fatal one,' Sean added leaning across the counter.

For a moment the Captain was stunned. 'Are you theatening me?' he asked incredulously.

'No,' Peter replied honestly. 'I'm promising you.'

For a moment the Captain was silent, remembering bitterly the final words of his briefing. 'You can expect every assistance from the local police.'

'You'd better stay here,' he told Peter. 'I'll take the Sergeant Major.'

Peter shrugged his shoulders and climbed back onto the counter. 'Either way,' he warned bluntly, 'if Terick gets shot,

113

you'll have that accident. I was going to be best man at his wedding.'

'So he was,' Sean seconded. 'And if anybody can arrange an accident in the bush, he can. Like a snake down your sleeping bag.'

The Captain walked towards the door, then he turned. 'Look, I can imagine how you feel, but see it from my side,' he asked. 'I'm a professional soldier. You can call me a professional killer if you like,' he added bitterly, 'other people do. I don't know this bloke, Terick, from a bar of soap. All I know is that he's killed a hell of a lot of people already, and I've got to stop him killing any more. You know that if I can take him unhurt I'll do it, but, if it comes to the choice between him or any of my men, he loses. I've no right to risk my men's lives any other way.'

He glanced across their faces hoping they would understand. But they did not. He shook his head and went to join his troops.

'Tell me if you see that big bloke hanging around,' he said to his sergeant.

'Yes, sir. Why sir?' the sergeant asked.

The Captain shrugged his shoulders uncomfortably. 'Nothing. I just want to know, that's all.'

CHAPTER TWENTY-THREE

KATCHEMU shook me gently awake. 'What time is it?' I asked sleepily.

'Full light,' Katchemu answered.

I lay still for a moment. I was so tired. Then I shook myself awake and crawled out of the cave. Katchemu was tending a fire, almost hidden by the shelter of a ledge below the kopje. He kept glancing up at the sky as he worked.

'There's rain coming,' he grunted as I joined him. 'Plenty, you can smell it.' The clouds were only specks in the distance but the air was moist and heavy.

I nodded towards the rising sun. 'Perhaps the heat will keep them away,' I said hopefully.

Katchemu shook his head. 'The rain will come,' he said certainly. 'Maybe at noon or just after. But first we must eat plenty of hot food, for this is the last fire we can have. The men ahead know that we are following them. They will watch out for us now because they cannot let us get close to their base camp.'

He handed me a tin to open. 'They will probably leave one man behind,' he continued, 'one man in the centre to help him, and one man goes on in front. Then they will move back past each other. That way all the time they are going forward they can ambush us as we follow. At night they'll make three camps so that we cannot attack them at once. And if we attack one the others can help him from behind.'

'Well, what are we going to do then?' I asked.

'Mambo, I have a plan,' Katchemu grinned, 'a very good plan.' He drew out his knife. I noticed that he didn't move his right arm. 'We are here,' he said marking the sand. 'Now we will move very quickly around to the river bed like this.' He drew a shallow curve with his knife. 'Then we will move backwards, like this.' He drew a straight line. 'It's simple,' he chuckled evilly. 'Each man will be protecting the man behind and not the man in front. As we move backwards we will kill each man as he comes forwards.' He looked across at me his eyes dancing. 'Is it a good plan Mambo?' I nodded, then I grinned at him.

'Let me have a look at your arm,' I asked. I pulled back his shirt before he could move away. The shoulder and arm were swollen, almost bursting the rough bandage, and the wound gave off a sweet sickly smell. His chest was the same. I looked at him. 'The disease has come.'

He nodded. 'It was bad luck,' he said philosophically. 'The knife must have been dirty.'

'Or poisoned?' I asked.

Katchemu shook his head. 'If that was so I'd be dead now.'

'You will be if the disease goes further,' I warned. I knelt beside him. 'Katchemu you must go back now while there is still time.'

Katchemu shook his head. 'I will fix the disease after we have eaten. I know a way,' he reassured me. 'It will be all right then. Besides,' he asked, 'what of you if I leave you. Beside these men you are like a child in the bush. They will kill you too quick.'

'There are only three now,' I answered confidently. 'I will catch them one by one, like the plan. A man who has as much hate as I do in his belly does not die easily.'

'Hate is no good against a machine gun. I go with you,' Katchemu said angrily. 'It was meant to be that way.' Suddenly he relaxed and grinned. 'Besides, my Mambo,' he urged, 'no man who is a hunter would miss the last kill. When it comes I have promised I will be there.'

We cooked up everything we had and sprinkled it with curry powder to hide the taste. Then we gorged ourselves like animals, because we knew that we would not eat again until the last terrorist was dead.

When we had finished Katchemu stood up. 'I go to find the muti,' he announced. 'Will you take all our water and make it hot?' He glanced up. 'We can fill the bottles again when the rain comes.'

He returned in about half an hour with various leaves, shrubs and the cuttings of bark from certain trees. He put them all in the pot and stirred it while it boiled. I did not have much faith in his muti and so I added all our salt until it became a thick murky grey brine.

At last Katchemu pronounced himself satisfied. He muttered a few half-remembered incantations over the brew and then spat in it. I cut away the bandages and as much of the congealed blood as I could.

'It'll be cool enough in maybe fifteen minutes.'

'No,' Katchemu muttered, 'put it on now.'

'Like this?' I asked.

Katchemu nodded. 'It works better this way.'

I wrapped a piece of my shirt-tail tightly around a small stick and dipped it in the pot. Then I pushed it into the wounds until the grey evil-smelling muti mingled with the fresh blood. Katchemu clenched his teeth as the heat and the brine worked into the wounds. He did not wince or make a sound, but beads of sweat ran down his grey face.

Again and again I sponged fresh muti across his chest and into his upper arm, until Katchemu pushed the stick away.

'It is enough now,' he gasped. He lay back and rested for a moment. Then he said, 'Take a flame from the fire and hold it to the wounds until the bad flesh burns away.'

'What?' I asked aghast.

'The flame,' Katchemu said.

'No,' I said, 'there must be some other way.'

Katchemu nodded. 'Some men take the white maggot and put it in the wounds and let them eat the flesh. I prefer the flame.'

He closed his eyes. 'Now,' he said. 'In another moment I may not be so brave.'

I poured a little paraffin onto a stick and lit it in the fire. Then I pushed it as deep as it would go into the wound in Katchemu's arm. The fresh blood boiled and the charred skin began to blacken and flake away. I held it there until Katchemu started to moan in a hoarse whisper through his clenched teeth. Then I poured some more paraffin on the stick and drew the flame slowly across Katchemu's chest.

Suddenly I heard the beat of helicopter blades racing towards me. I would have heard them long before if I had not been totally absorbed in holding the burning stick steady. The paraffin fire on the sand itself gave off no smoke, but burning drops had fallen from the stick and set the bush grass around us alight. The helicopter was racing towards the smoke.

I leapt up and began to beat out the fire. 'Katchemu,' I shouted, 'helicopter, take cover.' But Katchemu had fainted. The fire was spreading too fast for me to control. The helicopter was almost overhead. I seized Katchemu and dragged him farther into the overhang of the rock, and crouched beside him out of sight from the air.

The helicopter, with its nose down, swept over the rocks, rising and falling like a ship going through a heavy sea. Then it stopped, hovering above us, its blades almost touching the rocks. The beat from the engine made my ears sing, and the long stems of grass in its dark shadow swayed wildly in the down draught.

'He couldn't have seen us,' I prayed. 'He must think that it's an ordinary grass fire and just come to investigate.' Katchemu stirred beside me. The helicopter rose, still hovering above us, but the beat of the engine grew less. I breathed a sigh of relief.

Suddenly there was a harsh metallic crackle, then the sound of a voice came floating down.

'Hurndell. Show yourself. We know you're hiding here.'

I did not move.

'Hurndell,' the voice came again, 'there are SAS troops in the area searching for you. Give yourself up.'

'What's happening?' Katchemu asked, only just conscious.

I pointed to the shadow of the helicopter and his eyes widened with surprise. 'What do they want?'

'Us,' I answered grimly.

The helicopter turned and began to move slowly over the rocks, the voice repeating the message. I remembered the pot still boiling over the fire and our kit beside it.

'Katchemu, are you strong enough?' I asked. 'We've got to move. He knows we're round here somewhere. He'll keep looking for us until he can pin us down.'

Katchemu nodded. I cut off the lower half of my shirt and tore it into strips. Then I crawled out to the fire. Wide areas of grass were aflame now, sending showers of sparks and billows of white smoke skywards, while the helicopter roared continuously overhead searching for us amongst the rocks. I dipped the strips of shirt into the muti and collected our rifles, ammunition and water-bottles I left the packs behind. They would be useless weight from now on, anyway.

As quickly and efficiently as I could, I bound up Katchemu's wounds. Then, using both our belts, I strapped his arm securely to his side. He stumbled to his feet, sweat still pouring from his face. The pain must have been excruciating. I tried to reason with him again but he only shook his head determinedly. Then, using the cover of the dense smoke, we slipped quietly away.

'The helicopter's coming back, sir.'

The Captain glanced up from the table on which were spread various maps of the surrounding area.

'Thank you sergeant. I'll be out in a moment.' He rose, pushing the maps aside. They were useless to him. The Devil's Playground had been left blank. Nobody had bothered to chart it.

He walked slowly towards the landing area. The black speck loomed larger in the sky until the helicopter swooped down and came to rest on a narrow patch of grass. The pilot cut the engine and the blades started to slow. A supply Land Rover edged closer and the men began to unload jerry-cans of petrol.

When the revolving blades had nearly stopped, the pilot jumped out and hurried, crouching automatically, towards the Captain. Already the men had formed a human chain and were passing jerry-cans along to refuel.

'Hey! I know where they are,' the pilot said cheerfully.

'Where?'

'About twenty miles over there,' the pilot pointed. 'Give me a map and I'll show you.'

'I haven't got a bloody map,' the Captain said moodily. 'I tell you this bloody place hasn't been discovered yet. Did you see them?'

The pilot shook his head. 'No. Saw their cooking fire and their kit lying beside it. The wind from the blades must have spread the fire, 'cause the whole bloody area caught alight. I tried to pin them down, but they must have given me the slip under the cover of the smoke.'

'How long before you can take off again?'

The pilot shrugged his shoulders. 'Depends how fast your men can refuel.'

'Sergeant,' the Captain shouted over his shoulders, 'get those men working.'

'Yes, sir,' the sergeant shouted back. 'Hurry it up. Come on, hurry it up. Baker,' the sergeant roared at a man sitting in the shade of a Land Rover, 'get off your fat backside and hoist a jerry-can.'

'Runner,' the Captain shouted.

An African detached himself from the chain. The Captain scribbled a short note on a message pad, giving his grid map position and the direction and the distance of the sighting. He tore it off, placed it in an envelope and sealed it with a piece of wax.

'Take this to the police,' he ordered. The runner set off in a long, easy trot.

The sergeant came up. 'Ready, sir.'

'How many can you take?' the Captain asked.

'A stick of four with kit,' the pilot replied uneasily. 'But I tell you it's no joke. The bloody air currents in these rocks play havoc with my 'copter. It frightens me silly and I'm used to it, so I don't know what it's going to do to you and your men.'

'Just as long as you get us there. Where's the nearest landing area?'

'I think I can get down about quarter of a mile away. If not, the next likely place is about three miles away. I'll take you over and show you the place where I spotted them first so that you can find it again.'

They climbed into the helicopter. The pilot gunned the engine. He turned round to his anxious passengers. 'All ready?' he shouted cheerfully. They nodded grimly. 'Well here we go for a bumpy ride. Make sure your seat belts are tight. I don't want you falling out. Hate writing reports.'

'I wish you'd shut up,' the Captain said from between his clenched teeth as he fingered his safety belt.

'Just putting you in the mood,' the pilot replied cheerfully. 'It might be a bit of a struggle taking off with this load, so keep an eye on the rotor blade your side will you? Don't want them hitting a rock.'

The Captain did not answer. He was watching the rotor blades dipping under the weight as the helicopter lumbered uncertainly into the air.

The pilot had not exaggerated. The air currents tossed the helicopter about the sky like a ping-pong ball. The soldiers clutched at their seats while the pilot kept up a cheerful patter throughout the journey, because, as he explained, it kept his mind off it, otherwise he would probably wet himself.

The pilot banked the helicopter sharply then hovered some hundred feet above the ground.

'That's where I saw the kit,' he pointed. 'Now we'll take a compass bearing to the landing area.'

A few minutes later a tiny patch of open grass came into sight. The pilot pointed downwards with his thumb and the helicopter began to settle.

' 'Fraid you'll have to jump the last eight feet,' he shouted as he brought the helicopter to a hover. The Captain raised his arm and let it fall. One by one his men jumped out, and the helicopter lurched drunkenly from side to side as they left.

'Will you run a shuttle service for the others?' the Captain shouted. The pilot nodded and the Captain jumped.

The helicopter rose above him and disappeared over the rocks.

CHAPTER TWENTY-FOUR

'Where are we going?'

'To the terrorist camp,' Katchemu grunted. 'I want to see their spoor before we go on to the river bed.'

'Why? We've lost enough time already!'

'It is better to be careful with these men.'

We trudged on in silence until we came to the clump of fever trees. Katchemu began to cast around the camp. He frowned when he saw traces of his blood, dried black in the dust, and the signs of the fight around it.

'That one,' he snarled, 'died too easily.'

Suddenly, at the edge of the camp, he beckoned me to him impatiently. He pointed to some tracks leading off into the bush and the trail of dried blood that ran with them. He squatted beside the tracks and separated the blood from the dust. Then he broke it into a black powder with his fingers, studied it for a moment, and smelt it.

'It is difficult,' he said at last sitting back on his haunches. 'When the blood is fresh you can tell how bad the wound is by the colour. If it is bright red then the man is dying, for the blood is coming from the heart. If it is dull blood then maybe the wound is not so bad, for the blood had already been used. This blood is now old and it is therefore difficult to tell.' He looked up. 'But I think the man is dying. We will follow and see.'

We moved cautiously along the trail, Katchemu tracking some twenty yards in front, while I followed on higher ground to cover him against an ambush. After a quarter of a mile he stopped. I quartered the ground above him. There was no one hiding there. Then he beckoned me down to join him.

He pointed to the terrorist lying sprawled on his stomach beneath a rock, loosely hidden by grass. 'Your bullet,' Katchemu whispered. 'In the chest. He was strong to have walked so far.'

'The other tracks have gone on.'

Katchemu nodded.

'I don't know their uniforms but this one's probably the section leader. Maybe he has some papers.' I started forward but Katchemu reached out and stopped me.

'There is something wrong,' he said, 'I can feel it. The way they've hidden him. The way he lies.'

'Booby trap?' I asked, remembering the last incident with the grenade.

'Maybe,' Katchemu said uncomfortably. 'Maybe. These people are clever.'

We carefully checked the ground around the body, looking for loose threads leading from his clothes to a buried grenade. There was nothing, but Katchemu was still unhappy.

I lay down beside the terrorist and felt under his cold stiff body. There, under his stomach, I felt a grenade. They had placed it so that his weight held the trigger mechanism closed, but as soon as he was moved the grenade would explode. I found a second one under his thighs.

'Anything?' Katchemu asked anxiously.

'Two,' I answered. My arm was wet with body fluid.

'Leave him, Mambo,' Katchemu urged. 'It's too dangerous. We don't need the papers anyway.'

I stood up. Several hyenas were watching us from the safety of the rocks, awaiting their turn at the kill.

'He was stronger than we thought,' I said softly. 'They cut his throat to help him on his way.'

Katchemu shrugged his shoulders. 'Mambo,' he said simply, 'when man hunts or is hunted he must become like an animal, for only the strongest can live. Listen,' he said, 'if you are hunting a man and between you is a herd of game, well you must cross downwind otherwise the game will start and give you away. The man you hunt knows this and he is waiting for you. So you find the dung piles of the game and you cover yourself in it, all of you. Then you cross upwind and they cannot smell you. Then you catch the man from behind. And remember Mambo, a wise man always kills his quarry twice, then he is sure.

'Now these men were wise to kill this one, for he made them go slow and we could follow the trail of his blood easy. They are frightened of us now. But they are still very strong men and we must be careful of them.'

I listened quietly to his lecture. Then I nodded. 'I'll remember,' I said softly.

'Good,' my teacher grunted. 'Then perhaps we'll live long enough to kill these men.'

I took a compass bearing on the river bed. Katchemu stood in line with the needle.

'Now that they are only two,' he said, 'they won't try to ambush us, so look at your shadow. See which side it is as you face the river bed, and watch how it lies. As the sun grows higher your shadow will move. As we run watch always the sun and your shadow and you will run straight and fast, and not keep stopping to look at your compass.'

'They must be many miles in front by now,' I said anxiously.

Katchemu shook his head. 'They have had no sleep. They must rest sometime today, then we'll catch them.'

We started off in an easy loping trot, but every step jarred Katchemu's arm, and after a few yards he had to stop. He leant weakly against a rock, blood pumping through the bandages on his arm.

'The pain,' he admitted through his clenched teeth. 'It's too much. I have to go slower.'

Suddenly from behind us came an earsplitting crack and the startled shout of a man. Several more shouts answered him, and then the sound of FN rifles on automatic fire spraying the bush.

I scrambled up a high rock and spread myself out on its top. Below me I could see the small figure of a soldier standing by the terrorist. The shattered remains of a hyena lay nearby. A whistle blew and I saw a wide half-circle of troops sweeping swiftly through the bush towards us. A second half-circle of men walked a hundred yards behind so that no one could blast his way through. The men on the outer edges of the pincers were no more than half a mile away and were closing in fast.

I helped Katchemu up and he lay beside me. He watched them for a moment. 'Mambo,' he said suddenly, 'these men are looking for us, not the terrorists.'

I nodded.

'Why?' he asked bitterly.

I did not have time to explain for I heard the clatter of the helicopter in the distance.

We scrambled down the rock and flung ourselves behind the cover of some bushes. Seconds later the helicopter passed overhead. It banked sharply a mile past us. Then it turned back and began to sweep slowly back and forth in front of the searching men.

Katchemu grabbed my arm. 'Mambo, we must move. Now. Quickly . . . to a place where there are many rocks. We can hide there.' He started to run. After a few hundred yards I caught up and stopped him.

'Your blood. It's falling on the trail.'

'Bind it then,' he answered, gasping with pain. 'We must move quickly.'

I tore off my shirt and tied it tightly around his arm. If it did not stop the bleeding at least it would soak up most of the blood. I took his shotgun, ammunition pouch, and his water-bottle and slung them over my shoulder.

He glanced up at the darkening sky. 'Rain,' he pleaded. 'Please rain come now.'

We started to run again, measuring the yards to each possible cover in case the helicopter should come back. In the distance we could hear the excited blasts of a whistle relaying orders as they found our new trail.

I kept glancing up at the sky. At least we were running into the storm. The low dark clouds were racing towards us, and the thunder rumbled sullenly amongst them. After a mile Katchemu was sobbing with pain. I ran beside him and tried to help him but he shook me off. We turned sharply across a stretch of fairly open ground and into an area where the rocks lay so thick that we had to climb between them. The blast of a whistle told us that the troops were now no more than a quarter of a mile behind.

'Rain,' I sobbed, panting for breath. 'Oh, let it rain before it's too late.' As if in answer the heavens opened and the rain came down in blinding clouds. We turned again sharply and headed off at right-angles to make sure that they would lose our trail. Then Katchemu collapsed against a rock. Visibility was down to five yards except when the lightning forked. I stumbled up to him. The rain soaked through my shirt around his arm diluting the blood, and his whole side ran red. I pulled his good arm over my shoulder and staggered with him to the shelter of an overhanging rock.

'I'm going to find better cover for us,' I shouted above the noise of the storm. I laid him gently back and tried to make him comfortable. He slowly opened his eyes. They were full of pain, yet he smiled as he saw me fussing over him and he touched my arm.

'Go now, my Mambo. Find the cover.' Suddenly he chuckled. 'I never thought to see you acting like a young wife.'

I stood back and grinned at him. 'How's the pain, old savage?'

He shook his head. 'It is nothing, only I slipped back there. That's why I fell. If I rest for a few moments I'll be strong again.'

I nodded gravely. 'Katchemu is a giant,' I agreed. 'With one hand he can reach out and crush half the world.'

Katchemu nodded. Then he looked up and saw that I was teasing him and he grinned. 'Go now, my Mambo,' he said softly, 'before the strength comes back to the giant and he reaches out with his good hand and crushes you.'

I laughed, but I loved the courage of that man.

Constant peals of thunder vibrated through the rocks and the lightning forked down from the clouds. Cold driving rain matted the Captain's hair and stung his eyes.

'Bugger it,' he shouted, almost crying from rage and frustration. 'Bugger it, bugger it, bugger it.'

His sergeant came up. 'Connelley, in the advance patrol, reports that all tracks ahead have been washed out sir.'

'Do you realize, Sergeant,' the Captain shouted, 'if it wasn't for this bloody rain we'd have had 'em in another ten minutes? Then we could have all gone home. God, how I hate this bloody place.'

'Yes, sir,' the sergeant replied. 'What orders now, sir?'

The Captain took a grip of himself. 'Where were the tracks last seen heading?'

'Across a fairly open stretch of ground, sir. Looks as though they were heading towards a thick area of rocks.'

The Captain took a few impatient steps forward, then he spun round. 'They'll have gone to earth in there,' he said. 'Now we'll have to search every nook and cranny in the place. How big is the area?'

The seargeant shrugged his shoulders. 'I caught a glimpse of it before the rain came, sir. Looks about four hundred yards wide and about a quarter of a mile deep. But it's really thick stuff, sir.'

'Get the men back and throw a cordon around the place. Put a few snipers with binoculars on the tallest rocks to plug any gaps. We'll move as soon as the rain eases,' the Captain paused. 'No, Sergeant, we'll move in now.'

'But you can hardly see an inch in front of you, sir.'

'That's why they won't be expecting us, and they won't have time to find good cover. Well, get on with it sergeant. Don't just stand there.'

'Yes, sir.'

'Wait,' the Captain called after him. 'Did you find the man who shouted, and the others that fired?'

'Yes, sir,' the sergeant tapped his breast pocket. 'I've got their names in here.'

'Good,' the Captain said viciously, 'because they mucked the whole thing up and I'll have them for it when we get back if it's the last thing I do. They're supposed to be the finest bush troops in the country and they behave like children on a Sunday School picnic. Well, that's all. Get on with it, sergeant. I want those men in position and moving through the rocks in fifteen minutes.'

'Yes, sir,' the sergeant answered and bolted into the rain.

'Corporal White,' he called.

A figure came running up. 'Yes, Sarge.'

'Pass the word to get the men back here on the double.'

'Right, Sarge.'

'And I mean on the double, Chalky.'

'What's the matter?' the corporal asked anxiously. 'Captain got blood pressure?'

'Christ, you should see him,' the sergeant confided. 'He's dancing round the place like a camel with its bloody hump on fire. So snap to it.'

Katchemu was sitting upright under the ledge impatiently awaiting my return.

'There's lots of small caves,' I reported as I crawled in beside him. 'They're not much use though. They're too easy to spot. But about a couple of hundred yards from here there's a shallow dip with a clump of bamboos growing in it. It's acting as a natural pool for the rain water and it's filling up fast. I thought that we could cut a couple of pipes and try the old trick of hiding under water.'

'What are these soldiers like?' Katchemu asked.

'They're the best in the country.'

Katchemu shook his head. 'Mambo it won't work. They'll be looking for things like that.'

'How much longer do you think the rain will last?'

Katchemu looked up, trying to gauge the strength of the storm. 'Maybe half an hour more. Maybe twenty minutes. When it goes it will go fast.'

'Well, look, we can't stay in here even if they do miss us when they sweep. They'll soon pick up our trail, and with the helicopter we'll find it hard to shake them off. But if we go through them now there's just a chance that in the storm we'd get away with it. Then the rain will wash out our trail and we'll disappear. What do you think?'

Katchemu looked at me. 'Mambo, are you saying that we walk right into the jaws of the enemy? That's madness. These are not ordinary men. These are well-trained soldiers.'

I nodded excitedly. 'But they'll be cold and wet and miserable, and they won't be expecting us.'

Katchemu's eyes twinkled. 'Mambo,' he said proudly, 'I think you're mad but then I like your madness.'

I took the lead and we moved cautiously forward. On the edge of the open ground I stopped and flattened myself against a rock to break my silhouette. Katchemu did the same. For a moment we stared into the rain, looking for movement. Then Katchemu touched my shoulder.

'I'm black and therefore harder to see in this. I'll go first. When I find where the soldiers are I'll come back and tell you.'

I shook my head firmly. 'Wait, I'll go. You can't slither on your belly with only one arm.'

I dropped to my knees and crawled into the open ground. I had travelled this way for some twenty yards when a boot narrowly missed my hand. I froze and tried to bury myself in the mud.

'You there,' a voice roared above me. 'What's your name?'
'Jones, sir.'
'Well get into line. Sergeant.'
'Yes, sir.'
'Look at these men. Get them sorted out. I want each man ten paces apart, and the second wave ten paces behind and covering in the centre. Are the others ready?'
'Nearly sir.'
'Hurry it up.'
The boot moved.
'Number off,' the voice roared. 'Jones you start.'
'One ...' 'Two ...' 'Three ...' 'Four ...' 'Five ...' 'Six ...' 'Seven ...'

They were all around me, the voices receding into the distance as the numbers mounted.

I turned slowly and followed the trail, where my boots had scraped into the mud, back to Katchemu.

'They've got us cordoned off,' I breathed as I rose beside him.

'So we hide then,' Katchemu said.

'No,' I shook my head. 'If we hide they'll catch us. It's just a matter of time. We've got to get clean away. They're coming in ten paces apart and they'll be in two waves. So this is what we do.

'We'll fall back as they enter the rocks. Their lines are bound to grow ragged as they search. Then I'll get up and join in. You keep falling back in front of me. I'll go slowly and let the first wave overtake me. Then I'll join in the second wave and we'll do the same again. Once we're through you stop. I'll carry on for a little way then gradually I'll disappear and come back and join you.'

Katchemu beamed at me. 'Mambo,' he said. 'Your madness is too wonderful.'

We waited for about five minutes. Then Katchemu nudged me. 'They are coming.'

Grey figures were looming towards us through the rain and we began to fall back.

The first wave moved slowly through the rocks. They kept their bush hats pulled low over their eyes to protect them from the stinging rain, and they cursed their captain, their sergeant and the weather volubly, but they did their job well. Every rock every shallow cave was thoroughly searched. If we had chosen to hide they would have found us.

The difficult terrain made sure that their lines soon grew ragged. We found a spot where I judged that two soldiers were at least fifteen yards apart, and I stood up between them, some ten yards ahead and waited for them to catch me up. Then I moved forward with them.

Katchemu moved from cover to cover in front of me. One glimpse of his black skin would have given us away. I came to a small pool and began to poke at it with a stick. The others drew on ahead and I waited for the second wave to catch me up. A figure passed in front of me.

'You there,' it shouted and I recognized the voice. 'Don't think I'm not watching you. Get back into line. And put your bloody shirt on.'

'Sorry, Sarge,' I shouted. 'Just trying to keep something dry.'

The figure grunted and then moved on. The rain began to ease and my heart slowed with it.

'Keep moving,' Katchemu urged, 'or the ones coming from behind will see me. The rain'll come again stronger just now, but for the last time,' he warned.

I moved slowly on. Suddenly and with terrific force the wind howled through the rocks and the rain beat in gusts against my body. I stopped, poking with my stick in a crevice. The shadowy figures of the second wave slipped past me, bent almost double, their hats pushed down nearly at right-angles to protect their faces.

I moved forward with them, dropping one step for their two, until they disappeared. Then I turned and went to rejoin Katchemu.

We moved quickly. The water poured through the gaps in the rocks in torrents, and the mud churned underfoot. I stumbled around the side of a large rock and came face to face with a soldier sitting miserably in the mud.

'What's the matter?' I asked. Katchemu moved silently around the blind side of the rock.

The soldier nodded over his shoulder. 'Slipped while searching that bloody great rock. Reckon I've done my ankle in.

'What are you doing here?' he asked suspiciously.

'One of the blokes fell and cut his head open,' I lied easily. 'Bound it up with my shirt. It's not serious but the Sarge sent me back to get a stretcher. Can you walk?' I asked.

The soldier shook his head miserably. 'Broken, I reckon.'

'Well hang on there. I'll get help for you, too.'

'Mambo,' Katchemu said indignantly as I joined him, 'you can't leave that one. He may talk.'

'What do you want me to do? Kill him?'

'Yes. We can hide his body. They'll never find him.'

'No. We kill only the terrorists, and these men if we have to. But only if we have to. Do you understand?'

'Why? They come to hunt us with guns. We've done nothing to them. Why should we be gentle to them? Mambo, remember what I told you. Only the strongest live.'

'To kill without reason is not being strong. It's being stupid. That man lives. Look,' I said reasonably, 'by the time they find him they'll be in such a panic at having lost us that they'll just detail stretcher bearers and pack him off to hospital. He won't get a chance to query me even if he is suspicious.'

Katchemu grunted unconvinced.

'Which way shall we head?' I asked.

'Better to follow the storm fast for maybe two miles. Let the water wash out our trail. Then we circle back.'

'All right. You take the lead, but choose a pace that suits your arm. Here I'll take your kit.'

Katchemu shook his head. 'I can carry it,' he said stubbornly. 'I'm strong again now.'

CHAPTER TWENTY-FIVE

It was late afternoon. The shadows lengthened around the station in the gentle golden light of the setting sun, and a soft wind cooled the baked earth.

Ian stood by the window in the Member in Charge's office. 'It's hard to believe,' he said softly, 'standing here in all the quiet and the peace, knowing that sometime tonight I'll sleep and tomorrow I'll wake up and start again. Yet a few miles from here there are men hunting each other, living on their nerve ends. For them tomorrow may mean lying in the bush with a bullet in their belly watching the vultures circling overhead.'

Ian smiled. 'You've never heard me philosophizing before have you, Bill?' He leaned forward. His eyes caught a small cloud of dust in the distance racing towards them. 'There's a Land Rover headed this way,' he reported.

There came no reply.

Ian turned from the window. The Member in Charge was asleep, his head cradled in his arms on his desk. Ian shook him gently. 'There's a Land Rover coming this way from the rocks,' he said again.

The Member in Charge sat back, rubbing the sleep from his eyes.

'I could do with some coffee,' he said. 'Do you want some?'

Ian nodded. 'Better make it three cups. I've a feeling that's Captain Turnbull.'

'Constable,' the Member in Charge shouted.

Zacriah poked his head round the door.

'Bring coffee and three cups.' The Member in Charge turned to Ian. 'If it is, do you think he's got him? They had a good sighting and the helicopter.'

Ian shrugged his shoulders. Then the telephone rang shrilly. The Member in Charge picked it up.

'Bill, is that you?' came a stricken voice on the other end.

'Yes, sir.'

'Well, it's happened. I've just seen the reports from London. The whole bloody world's got the story,' the OC said bitterly. 'The headlines vary from "Mass Murder in Rhodesia – Policeman Goes Berserk" to "Wholesale slaughter of Africans. Rhodesian Police Force Goes Berserk". A well-known woman Cabinet Minister is demanding that British troops be sent immediately to restore law and order, and some of the Labour Dailies are organizing a relief fund for the victims' families. All hell's broken loose up here. I tell you the Minister's hovering at forty thousand feet. Have you got any news for me yet?' the OC asked anxiously.

'There's a Land Rover coming into the station now. We think it's Captain Turnbull. He may have something.'

'Well, look, in the meantime the Minister has declared your district a restricted area. There are reporters coming at you from all directions. We've just caught some of them chartering a private plane. The rest are coming down by road. Keep them out. Put up road blocks. Arrest them and stick them in cells if you have to. But keep them out. Do you understand?'

'Wouldn't it be better if we just told them the truth, sir?' the Member in Charge asked quietly.

'No,' the OC answered firmly. 'We've tried that before and we've found that the honest ones are very much in the minority.'

Captain Turnbull entered the office and slumped in a vacant chair. His uniform hung shapelessly around him and his face was drawn.

The Member in Charge put his hand over the telephone mouthpiece. 'What happened?' he asked.

'Lost them in a bloody rainstorm,' the Captain replied wearily. 'It's washed out all their tracks. They could be anywhere now.' He looked up. 'Who is it?' he asked.

'My OC,' the Member in Charge said.

'Flapping?' the Captain asked.

The Member in Charge nodded. 'Like a snared wild duck.'

'Oh God,' the Captain said.

The Member in Charge passed on the information to the OC. 'He's here, sir. Do you want to speak to him?' he asked.

'No,' the OC replied viciously. 'Let him tell it to his own HQ,' and rang off.

'Have some coffee,' the Member in Charge offered.

'Thanks,' the Captain said gratefully. 'I suppose the rain missed you here.'

'Yes,' Ian nodded.

The Captain leaned forward. 'I tell you I was so near him. It was just a matter of ten minutes. Then the heavens opened on me. He went to ground in some rocks, and I cordoned the place off. Then like a bloody fool I went and searched it in the rain. That must have been when he slipped away.'

'Men have escaped in much more difficult circumstances,' Ian said. 'Over prison walls or through the barbed wire and searchlights of prisoner-of-war camps. It's no fault of yours that you couldn't find them in a blinding rainstorm and in an area like the rocks which is almost impossible to search.'

The Captain shook his head. 'We searched it all right. It's just that I underestimated them. They must have slipped through us like a couple of ghosts. I won't make that mistake again,' he added ruefully.

The Member in Charge leant back in his chair. 'Which way was he heading?' he asked thoughtfully. 'I mean after the first sighting. Can you show me on the map?'

Captain Turnbull got up and walked over to the map. 'Here,' he pointed.

The Member in Charge opened a drawer in his desk and took out a pencil and some red-topped pins. He pressed one of the pins into the spot where the Captain indicated.

'And the first sighting was here?' he asked and the Captain nodded.

'The helicopter spotted them about here, and their first killing was about here.'

The Member in Charge drew a line along the pins and then stood back.

'I thought so,' he said after a while. 'Do you see there's a pattern. They may vary a bit when they make camp, but they always come back heading in the same direction. They must be on the terrorists' spoor, and the terrorists are probably heading for their base camp.'

'What lies beyond that?' the Captain pointed past the last pin.

'Nothing much,' the Member in Charge said. 'Oh yes, there is a dried-up river bed about here. Makes a pretty good landmark if you get lost. Winds through the whole area. You know,' the Member in Charge said suddenly, 'somewhere along that river bed is the most likely place for the terrorists to make their base camp. I mean, look at it. Easy access to the farming area on both sides. Ideal for moving supplies through.'

'So if I go back to the last point and then head in the same direction I might strike them?'

The Member in Charge shrugged his shoulders. 'Why not? It's a chance, but it's better than blundering aimlessly around the bush.'

'Right,' the Captain said decisively. 'That's what I'll do. Tell me,' he asked, 'any sign of the Bushmen yet?'

'Three of them,' Ian cut in. 'We sent them out to your camp about an hour ago. Poor bastards are frightened silly. One minute they're tracking game in Wankie and the next they're wafted up here. The helicopter was the last straw. Last I saw of them they were being sick over your pilot.'

The Captain made for the door. 'I suppose I'd better phone my HQ,' he said regretfully. 'I can't delay it much longer.'

'Leave it,' the Member in Charge put it kindly. 'I'll do it for you. I'll tell them you're on a new lead.'

'Thanks,' the Captain said from the bottom of his heart. 'Oh, by the way we found two more bodies. One was booby-trapped and blew to pieces so we just buried what we could find. The other we're bringing in. We found him in a cave. He was tortured and his throat was cut. Looks like this bloke of yours has really turned vicious.'

'They tortured his fiancée to death. How would you behave if you were him?' Ian asked quietly.

The Captain did not reply.

'You'd better go carefully,' the Member in Charge warned softly. 'He's pretty desperate. He'll probably shoot you if you come between him and the albino.'

'I will,' the Captain assured him. 'I will. Seeing what he did to that terrorist shook me rigid. You haven't seen Peter, have you?' he asked worriedly.

The Member in Charge looked up. 'I thought he was with you.'

'He's not. Find him, will you, and keep an eye on him.'

'Why?'

'I don't want a snake down my sleeping bag,' the Captain said, and closed the door behind him.

'What does he mean?' Ian asked. The Member in Charge shrugged his shoulders.

CHAPTER TWENTY-SIX

Dusk was gathering as we reached the dried-up river bed. We branched off into the rocks and again made camp high up in a kopje. I was worried about Katchemu. It seemed as though he was starting a fever.

The crescent moon and the stars shone down from a cloudless sky. We crouched on either side of the narrow entrance to the cave, facing each other, our backs against the still warm rock. The temperature was dropping fast and we had little clothing with which to protect ourselves. It was going to be a long, cold night.

I tried to take stock of the situation. We had plenty of water and the rain pools in the rocks would last for another two days. We had no food but that was not important.

'How many cartridges have you got left?' I asked.

Katchemu tapped his shotgun. 'Five in here and three spare.'

'I've got twelve rounds left. Not many against machine guns.'

Katchemu shrugged his shoulders philosophically. 'Their ammunition must be going faster than ours. Besides, we can still use our knives. A knife is better against a man you hate. When you bury it in him you can see the life leave his body.'

'Do you want me to try and re-bind your wounds?' I asked.

Katchemu shook his head. 'Better to leave it,' he said. 'If it is clean a knife wound heals better in its own blood.'

'Is there still much pain?'

'No, there is nothing,' Katchemu replied and I knew that he was lying.

I put my arms around my legs and rested my body on my knees, trying to hold the warmth in my body. 'Katchemu,' I asked softly, 'do you feel a great loneliness? I do. I feel it more now than the pain and anger. I miss my Madam so much, Katchemu. Even as we march I think of her. How she smiles. How her hair moves with the wind. I think of so many things that I wanted to tell her. During the night I try to reach out and touch her, to feel her comfort me. Then I wake up and there is nothing... only the darkness and the smell of death.

'I lie in that dark and I know that I cannot go back, for the world that I had is no longer. And after I have killed the albino I cannot go forward because I have no world to go to. It is then that I feel this great loneliness empty in my belly. It moves against the anger and the pain, until these feelings swamp my mind, and I know that I am going mad. I call to my Madam in the darkness of my mind to help me, for I am drowning, but she cannot, Katchemu. Do you understand?'

'No, Mambo,' Katchemu shook his head sadly. 'For me a woman is like a cow. And many women are like many cattle. For me they are what I own. Not what I love. But I guard them and I care for them because they are mine. You are a European and therefore very stupid about these things.

'You loved only the Madam and you will love her all the days of your life. This I know and it makes me sad, my Mambo. Because you gave her too much. When she died she took your soul with her, and now you have nothing. It is better to love many things a little than one thing too much.'

'How can you say "I will love this a little or that a lot." It just happens. But I tell you Katchemu,' I said fiercely. 'I tell you that for all the pain I'm glad I loved her.'

We sat in silence then Katchemu asked softly, 'Mambo, why do these men hunt us?'

'Because in killing the terrorists we broke the law. You know that.'

'Even though they killed the Madam and burnt the farm?' Katchemu asked.

I nodded. 'Only the law can kill them.'

'So if we were still policemen and they had killed another madam, and we killed them, we would be all right?'

'Maybe, if we gave them a chance to surrender first.'

'And if they had surrendered, they would have been killed in jail for killing the other madam?'

'Yes,' I said.

'So they would have died anyway,' Katchemu continued doggedly.

I nodded.

'But when we kill these men who killed our Madam and burnt our farm, who are going to be killed anyway, they send men to hunt us.'

'It is the law,' I said.

'Oh Mambo,' Katchemu answered bitterly, 'the European is very strange. He has so many laws but he has so little justice.'

I shrugged my shoulders. 'Katchemu, I'm sorry I can't explain. I don't understand it myself. I know that the law was made by civilized men. Perhaps I'm not very civilized.'

'So what will happen when the soldiers catch us?' Katchemu asked.

'They will take us for trial. Maybe I will be hanged. You they will send to jail.'

'So your own people will hang you for killing the man who tortured your Madam to death?'

'No, if they hang me it is because I broke the law. And maybe because they're frightened that other men will do the same. I will serve as a warning.'

Katchemu thought for a moment. 'Mambo, are you afraid to die?' he asked softly.

I looked up. 'I don't think so,' I said slowly. 'Not after I have killed the albino. It'll be better than the loneliness.'

Katchemu nodded. 'Sometimes I have a loneliness, too. I fear age coming on me. And the world I love is changing. I am like a man one step behind. I fear to wait in a jail as my strength leaves me. I fear to sit in my age by a fire and eat gifts of food between broken gums. No,' he shook his head firmly, 'all the days of my life I have lived as a man. When the time comes I shall die like one, under the clear sky with the blood of anger running like fire through my veins. Is it the same for you?'

I nodded.

'Well, then, my Mambo, when you have killed the albino we can turn and fight the soldiers until we die. Then we go on a new journey, you and I. We will not be lonely together.'

'To another world,' I said softly, half to myself.

Katchemu heard me. 'Maybe you are thinking that your God will not like you killing the soldiers?' he asked.

'Something like that,' I agreed.

'Mambo, don't worry,' Katchemu reassured me. 'Once I spoke with the holy man at the mission. He told me that your God was once a man. He'll understand.'

I smiled at him. 'Go to sleep,' I said softly. 'We'll talk of this again after the albino is dead. I'll watch.'

In the early hours of the morning the cold became numbing. Katchemu was in terrible pain, grey-faced and sweating, shaking uncontrollably as the fever ate into him. I lay beside him and tried to warm his body with mine, until I could stand his agony no longer and I made a fire at the entrance to the cave. I knew that the light could be seen for miles around, but I did not care. I was sure that Katchemu was dying.

I pulled him over to the fire and sat with his head in my lap, wiping away the sweat from his eyes. He was murmuring to me in broken Sindebele, tugging weakly at my arm. But I couldn't understand him. I could only sit there watching helplessly.

Just before dawn his fever broke for a while and he seemed to fall into a semi-conscious sleep. I made a mattress of grass outside the cave and laid him where the rising sun would warm him. Then I stacked up the fire until billows of smoke rose.

The smoke would lead the troops to him and they would get him to hospital. A good lawyer would claim that his only fault was to follow me. I hoped that the judge would be lenient. Either way a few years in jail would be better than dying of fever, alone, on the barren side of a kopje.

I broke his beloved shotgun against a rock as a precaution. Then I glanced up at the sky. It was time for me to leave. I stood before him and raised my rifle in a silent salute.

'Thank you,' I said softly.

The side of the kopje was steep and slippery from loose stones. Around me I could just make out the blurred shapes of stunted trees and scattered boulders. In the cold harsh pre-dawn light I made a lot of noise, holding my rifle above my head in case I fell. Below lay an open stretch of ground and then the sharp dip of the dried-up river bed.

Suddenly there came a wink of scarlet flashes, then the dry stammer of a sub-machine-gun. I felt my arm jerk up, moved by some irresistible force, then fall helplessly to my side. A second burst screamed over my head and I felt the wind from the bullets.

I threw myself sideways and rolled down the slope, the bullets following me. I crashed into a boulder and lay there stunned for a moment, a shower of loose stones landing on top of me. Then I scrambled up. A burst spent itself amongst the stones where I had been lying. Another burst ricocheted off the top of the boulder by my head and screamed off into space.

I ducked and ran wildly across a few yards of open ground, to throw myself panting behind another cover. For a moment there was silence. I could hear cautious footsteps on either side as they closed in on me. I felt the wound. The bullet had torn a shallow furrow through the muscle. The blood dribbled down my arm and a white-hot pain was starting.

I changed my cover again. The noise brought on another burst. I threw myself against a rock and began to fire at the flashes. Sweat poured down my face, blurring my vision.

The shadow of a head bobbed up in front of me from behind a boulder. I fired at it and missed. It was my last round. The magazine was empty. I tore it off and tried to pump my remaining rounds into it with one hand. It's all over now, I told myself, and waited for the shock of their bullets to strike.

Instead their firing died. The helicopter came in low out of the rising sun, its blades whirling in a silvery arc above it. For a moment I thought of waving to attract its attention. Then I flattened myself out under the rock. It was none of their business.

The helicopter banked sharply to the right and came in again, pin-pointing the smoke from Katchemu's fire. One of the terrorists, realizing this, opened up with his sub-machine-gun. The helicopter started like a frightened rabbit, banked again, then scurried away. The terrorist's sub-machine-gun fell dejectedly silent. I heard the other cursing him in a high piping voice.

By this time I had crawled to a safer cover higher up, and clicked the magazine back into position. Then I waited with my rifle resting against the rock.

Below me there was silence, except for the occasional chink of a loose stone. Suddenly there came a burst of fire from both sides. The ground by the rock, behind which I had been hiding, dissolved into dust and screaming bullets.

Again there was silence as the dust slowly settled. The commissar broke cover and approached the rock. I heard his startled shout of warning when he found that I was gone. Then he spun round, knowing that he was exposed, desperately trying to sight me amongst the rocks. He saw the snout of my rifle training on his stomach from a few feet away, and his mouth split open in a silent scream of terror, his sub-machine-gun dangling uselessly by his side.

I squeezed the trigger. The hammer clicked forward then stopped at half-cock. In my hurry I had not rammed the bolt properly home and the cartridge had jammed. For a second we stood motionless. Then the commissar's lips curled into a smile and he slowly raised his sub-machine-gun.

'Don't shoot him yet,' the high piping voice ordered from behind. 'I want to talk to him.'

The commissar walked up to me and smashed the butt of his sub-machine-gun into my face. I fell backwards. He kicked me hard in the stomach. Then he leaned over as I lay squirming with pain and wrenched the rifle from my hands. He searched me expertly, taking my knife, and stood back.

'Bring him down here to the open ground and cover us,' the albino ordered.

The commissar dragged me to my feet and pushed me down the slope in front of him. I collapsed against a rock by the albino and slipped slowly down to a sitting position in front of him.

The albino tied my hands behind my back with strips of clothing. Then he drew a noose around my neck and tied it to my hands so that the slightest movement would strangle me.

He handed his sub-machine-gun to the commissar. 'Keep this,' he ordered, 'just in case he works free.'

The commissar grunted and moved back. He rested the second sub-machine-gun on the ground and leant up against a tree. The albino squatted before me, taking care to keep out of the line of fire.

'If you try to do anything foolish,' the albino said softly, 'I'll cut the tendons in your arms and legs and cripple you. I would have done it before but I'm afraid that the pain may make you faint, and I haven't the time to wait for you to come round again. You're surprised that my English is so good? I went to an excellent university,' he explained when I did not reply.

'Where is your companion?' he asked. 'Is he dead?'

'Yes,' I replied wearily.

'I thought so,' the albino nodded. 'It was very stupid of you to light that fire. I knew that you would have lost our trail in the rain so it confirmed my suspicion that my late radio operator told you where my base camp was. By the way he is dead, isn't he?'

'Very,' I answered savagely.

'I take it you tortured him?'

I nodded.

'He was useful to me,' the albino said. 'Before you die you will regret having done that. Who are you?' the albino asked suddenly. 'Why did you hunt us? You're not working with the police.'

I did not answer.

'Tell me,' the albino whispered, drawing the blade of his knife gently across my throat.

'You know Katchemu once described your face to me. He said it was like that of a rotting corpse who should have been buried many days ago.'

The albino's eyes flashed and I waited for his knife to tear into my throat. But he relaxed and then he sat back.

'No,' he said softly, reading my thoughts. 'You won't die that easily. I suffered too much while you were hunting me. Besides, I find my face an asset. It frightens people.' He leant forward. 'Does it frighten you?' He studied my face. 'No,' he said softly, 'I see there is too much hate in your eyes. Like those of a man on the verge of insanity. To you I would imagine death would come as a relief. Is it because of the girl?' he asked. He watched my eyes. 'Yes,' he breathed. 'I think so. She was very beautiful, wasn't she? What was she to you? Was she your mistress or perhaps even your wife? She was frightened of my face.' He smiled as he saw me wince. 'When she saw it she screamed and tried to break away. But my men held her.' His voice dropped to a hoarse whisper. 'Your woman had a skin that was soft to touch and so clean. She was brave, your woman. At first she was silent but then later she began to scream and scream and scream. You should have heard her,' he whispered. 'It was wonderful.'

'Your name is Terick, isn't it?' He moved nearer.

I lunged forward desperately trying to tear out his throat with my teeth. He laughed softly as I missed and lay writhing on the ground by his feet.

'I thought so,' he continued hoarsely. 'I thought so. Because in her agony she kept calling out your name. Again and again and again. But you weren't there to help her, were you? I could have been mistaken, though. It might have been the name of one of her other lovers that she was calling and I mistook it for yours. Tell me?' he asked, 'tell me their names and I'll try to remember for you.'

'Albino,' I shouted between my clenched teeth, for I was

shaking uncontrollably. 'You're dead. You died from the moment you touched her. If I don't get you, the soldiers will. Either way you're dead. I promise you that.'

The albino smiled, his lips half-twisting into a sneer. 'First we will talk more of your woman,' he whispered caressingly, 'and I will watch you slowly go mad. Then, and only then, will I kill you. As for me, well, you're the only one who knows where my base camp is. Those men that you killed are nothing. Stupid savages who are expendable. In the base camp I have a radio. When I get back I'll signal for more to come down. Then there'll be more farms and more women.'

A startled yell of warning from the commissar turned both our heads. Katchemu was crawling down the kopje. The commissar threw up his sub-machine-gun and fired wildly. Katchemu rose to his feet roaring with anger, his knife flashing in his hands, and staggered drunkenly towards the commissar, picking up speed with the slope.

It was so sudden. The albino and I stared motionless.

The commissar fired again and the first bullets ripped across Katchemu's chest. He bellowed with blind anger, staggering under the impact, but that giant of a man kept coming fast with his knife held out in front of him.

The second blast caught him when he was only ten feet away. His legs began to buckle. Blood ran freely down his chest. He fixed his red eyes on the commissar's face and his momentum kept him staggering on.

Six feet away, Katchemu's mouth split wide open. Blood frothed in bubbles on his lips as he yelled in exaltation at the kill. The commissar's nerve broke. He dropped his gun and threw his arms over his eyes, screaming, as Katchemu lunged forward. I saw the knife flash. Then it bit deep into the commissar's stomach until the hilt was buried and the blade went on into the tree.

For a moment they remained locked together. Then Katchemu buried his head in the commissar's chest and slid slowly down his crucified body to crumple at his feet, his hand reaching slowly out for the albino's sub-machine-gun.

The albino leapt up and in the same movement slashed at

my throat. I threw myself sideways. The knife missed and buried itself in my shoulder. Then the albino was gone, racing down the kopje towards the river bed.

For a moment I felt nothing. I just stared down at my shoulder. Then I felt the pain begin to burn, glowing hotter and hotter like a poker thrust into a fire. I gritted my teeth to stop myself from crying out as I sawed the thin strips of clothing against the edge of a rock until I freed my hands. Then I leaned back against the rock and using both hands I slowly drew the knife from my shoulder. Swirling clouds of red agony filtered through my brain and I heard myself cry out. Moments later I regained consciousness. The knife lay beside me. My body was bathed in sweat and my lungs were gasping for breath. I heard Katchemu groan. I clawed my way to my feet and staggered over to him.

His eyes were closed and his lips were twisted into a snarl. Blood dribbled from the corners of his mouth. I knelt beside him and his eyelids flickered open.

'The albino,' he breathed.

'I'll get him,' I promised. 'It'll be easy now.'

'I can't see you,' he whispered urgently and his hand reached out for mine.

I clutched his hand and held it tightly.

'I'm going now, Mambo,' he whispered. 'Don't be sad. There is no pain, only darkness. I can feel myself sinking.' His hand reached up and touched my face. 'That night when we talked in the cave,' he whispered. 'I lied. For I loved you, my Mambo. You were my mother and my father. I would have followed you anywhere.'

Suddenly he chuckled and the blood formed bubbles on his lips. 'Mambo, oh my Mambo,' he breathed, 'we hunted well together, you and I. They won't kill any more, those devils. Perhaps when we go on the new journey there'll be more hunting.'

A smile crossed his face as he died and his hand slipped slowly away from mine. I looked up. The sky was clear and flooded with sunlight. The air was fresh and clean.

'Goodbye, Katchemu,' I whispered. 'I'll miss you, you old

savage. Oh God, how I'll miss you. I loved you, too.' Then I rose and walked slowly away. Oh, God damn it. I was crying.

CHAPTER TWENTY-SEVEN

THERE came a knock on the office door and the duty sergeant entered.

'There is a runner come, Mambo,' he reported.

'Send him in, Matambo.'

The runner entered and came stiffly to attention, his chest heaving. He held out an envelope. The Member in Charge took it and broke the seal. Then he glanced up at the runner.

'Thank you,' he said. He turned to the sergeant. 'Take him out and give him all the skoff he wants.'

'Yes, Mambo,' the sergeant said and marched the runner out of the office.

The Member in Charge left his desk and walked over to the wall map, reading the message.

Ian entered the office with a mug of coffee in his hand. 'Your turn for breakfast,' he said. 'I'll look after things here. Why don't you get a few hours decent sleep as well? I'll call you if anything happens.'

The Member in Charge shook his head. 'It already has. Just got a message from Captain Turnbull. The helicopter spotted smoke at first light by the river bed. Went to investigate and got shot at. They think there's been another clash with the terrorists. The troops are closing in fast. But there's no place for the helicopter to land between them and the river bed.'

Ian whistled softly. 'Many dead?' he asked.

The Member in Charge shrugged his shoulders. 'Doesn't say. I don't suppose the helicopter hung around long enough to find out.'

'Well it's only a matter of time now,' Ian said. 'With the Bushman trackers Terick hasn't got a chance of shaking the troops off again.'

'I know,' the Member in Charge replied. 'Well, I suppose I'd better go and report the glad tidings to the OC. It'll make his breakfast taste better at any rate.'

CHAPTER TWENTY-EIGHT

'TERICK. Terick.' The voice shouted again. I crawled to the ledge of a rock and looked down from behind the cover of a boulder.

Peter was standing below me in a small depression. He was dressed for the bush with a rifle slung over his shoulder and a pack on his back. A battered hat shielded his eyes.

'Look, I know you're here,' he shouted. 'I picked up your trail.'

'Go away,' I shouted.

He spun round, trying to pick out the direction of my voice, as it echoed in the rocks that formed a wall around him.

'I found Katchemu,' he shouted with his back to me. 'You're all alone now.'

'So what do you want me to do?' I shouted bitterly. 'Give myself up?'

'No, you silly bugger,' Peter shouted desperately. 'I've come to help you. You've got the Army on your tail.'

'I know. How far behind?'

'Maybe two hours but they're closing fast and they've got Bushman trackers with them. Man, I tell you, you need me.'

'No. There's only the albino left and he's unarmed. I'll get him alone. It's private.'

'You're bloody mad. He'll lose you in the rocks.'

'Maybe, but I know where he's heading and I'll catch him. Now will you go, Peter. And Peter, if you try to follow me I'll shoot you in the legs. Friend or not. Do you understand?'

Peter nodded his head miserably, then he turned and faced me. 'What do you need?' he asked.

'Just some .303 ammunition if you've got it and some field dressings.'

'Why do you want the field dressings?' Peter asked suspiciously. 'Are you all right?'

'Yes, I'm fine. I just might need them, that's all.' I raised my rifle. 'Don't come any closer,' I warned.

'Who are you trying to fool?' Peter said softly. 'You've left a trail of blood from way back. Man, if you keep going you'll bleed to death.'

'The dressings'll slow it. Anyway I'll keep going long enough for what I want. Now, are you going to leave them or not?'

Peter unbuckled his cartridge belt and laid it on the ground. Then he shrugged off his pack and opened it.

'I've left you some food as well,' he said.

'Peter, when you leave, no tricks. I know that you can winkle me out of these rocks, but if you try I'll fight. I've got to get that albino alone.'

'Was he the one who tortured her?'

'Yes. He organized the whole thing.'

'All right, no tricks,' he promised. He looked up, trying to find more words, but they wouldn't come. 'Good luck,' he said softly. Then he walked away.

I waited for about ten minutes before I moved down to the equipment. I buckled on the cartridge belt and recharged my magazine. I had only two of my own rounds left. Then I cut away the rags that bound my wounds. The thick, half-congealed blood, suddenly released, oozed slowly down my side. I quickly unwrapped the field dressings and bandaged the more serious wound in my shoulder first. The remainder I used on my arm. Then I buried the rags and the food out of sight.

I glanced at my watch. It was half past seven. I had eleven

hours of daylight left. Peter had been right. I had followed the albino into the rocks and lost his trail.

An hour later I was jogging along the dried-up river bed. The sand was firm and dry and up to twenty feet deep in places, betraying no trace of the millions of gallons of water that flowed slowly some six feet beneath its surface.

The albino probably considered me dead or at least incapacitated, but he knew that the troops would be closing in, and that was why he had chosen the more difficult passage through the rocks, rather than the easier going of the river bed. The troops would certainly search the area surrounding the bodies and his tracks would stand out clearly in the firm sand. The extra time taken in tracking him through the rocks would grant him a few precious hours. Enough for a desperate man, alone and unarmed, without food or equipment, to get back to his base camp and hole up. But at some stage he had to cross the river bed which lay between him and his base camp. As I ran I was watching for his tracks.

Towards noon I found them. The bottom sand which he had kicked up was still damp from the recent rain. I sifted it through my fingers. The heat was evaporating the moisture quickly. I started after him and increased my pace. He was tiring for he had now chosen to run along the river bed, sacrificing caution for speed.

In another half-hour I spotted the albino at the far end of a long straight stretch. The river bed made a lazy U-turn and he disappeared from sight. I silently closed the gap to two hundred yards. The banks rose vertically ten feet on either side. In places the roots from trees, balanced precariously on the edge, twisted through and reached down into the sand.

The river bed began to straighten out again. I closed the gap to a hundred and fifty yards. He still hadn't heard me. He was running with his head down and his elbows working on either side. In the distance I could hear the strained rasp of his breathing.

I cocked my rifle, then I threw it up and fired. I felt the butt kick against my shoulder. A searing pain ran through my arm. The bullet whipped into the sand by the albino's feet. He spun round and saw me. Another bullet hummed past his face. He turned and began to run wildly, searching for a break in the banks, trying to widen the gap, waiting at any moment to feel the lash of a bullet in his back.

I closed to a hundred yards and fell in behind him, maintaining the distance between us. There was plenty of time. I would run him to death if I could.

Two hours passed. The afternoon sun burned down and reflected back off the white sand. We were staggering along at little faster than walking pace now. Sweat matted my hair and poured down my naked chest. Blood soaked through the field dressing and ran down my side and arm. My breath came in short racking sobs, while pain raced like fire through my body at every step.

Ahead of me the albino fell. He crawled for a few paces on his knees. Then he collapsed onto his face. I staggered up to him and stopped ten yards away resting on my rifle.

I tried to speak but the words dried in my mouth. I uncapped my water-bottle, poured some of it over my face and neck, then I swilled out my mouth repeatedly, taking care to drink only a little of the water and spitting the rest out.

The albino slowly raised his head. His sores had opened and his face was a mask of sand and sweat. His hand reached out, pleading for the water-bottle. I shook my head and replaced the cap.

'Run, you bastard,' I panted. 'Go on, run.'

'No,' the albino sobbed weakly. 'No, you shoot me now, I'm going no farther.' He let his head fall back into the sand.

I raised my rifle and steadied myself, for the sights were weaving before my eyes. I took careful aim then I squeezed the trigger.

The bullet cut like a whiplash across the albino's back above his shoulder blades. He screamed and started to his feet.

'Did she scream like that?' I panted. 'Now you . . . you run. And I'll be just behind you. Every time you stop there'll be another bullet. For her. For Katchemu. For my boys. For my farm. Oh, albino,' I panted, 'there are plenty of bullets.' He started to run.

Time passed. I don't know how long. The sun was dropping and it began to grow cooler. But we were dying, the albino and I, as we staggered along the river bed at less than a walking pace. Three scars lined his back for the times he had stopped and I left blood in my footprints.

He collapsed for the fourth time against one of the small rocks that littered the bed. His fingers clawed for a grip on its smooth surface. Then slowly he sank down to rest with his back against its base.

I staggered up to him and rested against a nearby rock.

'Kill me,' he screamed. 'Kill me. Kill me. Kill me. Kill me. Oh God,' he started to cry, 'why don't you kill me. No farther. No farther. You can shoot me to pieces but I'm not running any farther.'

'I'm giving you a chance,' I panted. 'That's more than you gave her. You're still alive and as long as you live you have the chance of finding some way of killing me or losing me. But you only have until the light fails. Then I'm going to kill you.'

'You're mad,' the albino sobbed. 'You're losing so much blood. Neither of us will get out of here alive.' He struggled to his feet and came towards me. 'You're supposed to be civilized,' he pleaded, 'yet you're running me to death like an animal. I don't understand. Is that what civilized men do?'

I jerked my rifle up. He darted forward screaming at the top of his voice, a stone raised in his hand. I waited until he was almost on top of me and then I fired. The stone fell to the sand. The albino stopped as though paralysed, the scream dying on his lips. Slowly he looked at his shattered hand.

'Oh God,' he choked. 'Oh God, oh God, oh God.'

'Run,' I panted, 'run.'

The albino turned and staggered off, holding his injured arm across his chest.

The blood-red sun began to set and its rays, where they fell on the sand by my feet, ran in rivers of shimmering scarlet. In a quarter of an hour the light would fail.

Ahead the pool came into sight and a place where the game had broken down the banks to drink. The albino began to edge towards the broken bank. As he drew level he put on a sudden spurt, clambered up the slope and disappeared into the rocks. I followed him and closed to twenty yards.

We began to ascend the kopje, climbing and falling and crawling over the boulders and rough ground. Up and up and up, our mouths wide open, our tortured lungs screaming for breath as we used every last desperate ounce of energy.

Once he turned and tried to roll some boulders onto me but he was not strong enough to move them and he had to carry on, while I gained another five yards.

At last he collapsed on a narrow ledge halfway up. The light was failing fast. I climbed up close to him. His eyes, like two great, red-rimmed pools of darkness against his grey mottled face, watched mine.

He wearily glanced upwards. 'Another two hundred yards and I'd have reached the cave. Then you'd have been dead. Dead!' He spat at me.

I swung the barrel of my rifle and pointed it at his chest. 'And now you,' I panted.

His full, pink lips, cracked with heat, split into a snarl like a livid scar across his face. 'You can only kill me,' he panted, 'but you can't get back your woman or your farm or your boys. I took those from you. You'll never forget the way she died. She was beautiful, your woman.' His long, white, skeleton-like fingers began to caress the bloodstained folds of his filthy white robe. 'So soft,' he whispered. He looked up and smiled at the torment in my face. 'I never had a white woman before.' His eyes widened with excitement.

I dropped my rifle and drew out my knife.

'They held her down for me,' he breathed, 'then I . . .'

I lunged forward. We scuffled on the ground for a moment. His voice rose to a quivering scream. Higher and higher and higher until it broke. I watched him bleed to death. Then I dragged his body to the ledge and let it roll down the side of the kopje.

CHAPTER TWENTY-NINE

THE pilot entered the office. The Member in Charge looked up.

'What do you want?'

'Well, some coffee will do,' the pilot replied cheerfully, 'but I'd prefer some decent food. These ration packs may be all right for the Army, but they play havoc with the Air Force's digestion. My 'copter's US,' he explained. 'Broke down early this morning after I saw the smoke. Had to wait for a lift back with the supply Land Rover.'

Ian looked up interested. 'So the sub-machine-gun did get you.'

The pilot shook his head. 'No, nothing as exciting as that I'm afraid. Just mechanical failure. I'll have to phone through for some replacement parts. Oh, by the way, they've got that bloke of yours.'

'Where?' both the Member in Charge and Ian asked, starting to their feet.

'Well they haven't actually got him yet,' the pilot admitted, 'but he's on a kopje. 'Bout here,' he pointed on the map. 'When I left they were cordoning it off. They'll probably be moving in about now. Captain Turnbull's taking no chances this time. That bloke hasn't got a snowball's chance in hell.'

The Member in Charge and Ian were looking at the map. The Member in Charge made a circle of pins around the supposed site of the kopje. Then he drew a line from the last sighting.

'Well,' the Member in Charge said softly, 'he gave them a run for their money.'

I gathered wood for a fire. I was tired and weak and I moved slowly. The base of the kopje was surrounded by a ring of flaming torch brands winking in the distance below me, like cigarette ends in the dark. There came the faint shrill of a whistle and the ring began to move slowly up the slopes.

I made a fire on the ledge. The light would soon guide them to me. Then I charged the magazine and tested the action of my rifle. I meant to let them get close, then a few shots over their heads and it would soon be over.

I leant drowsily back against the rock watching the flames dancing in the fire, reaching up into the night. The heat warmed my body and a great feeling of peace stole over me.

I tried desperately to remain conscious as the last moments of my life ticked away, to persuade my eyes to focus on the flaming ring of torches as the troops closed in on me. Perhaps it was from the loss of blood, or perhaps the steel had left my soul, for my head slowly dropped to rest on my knees and my mind began to wander.

A soft night wind sprang up and moaned across the rock face of the kopje, making the sparks leap from the fire. Oh, Sally. I called to her softly in the darkness of my mind. It's Saturday. This afternoon we were to be married. Tonight all the world will be at parties, couples swaying to the music in the shadows of a crowded room. And I. I wait here alone, wishing so hard for you to be with me.

A moment's sadness and then I smiled, for I thought I saw Katchemu materializing before me in the path of the rising moon. In one hand he held his beloved shotgun, high above his head in greeting. He pointed and suddenly I saw Sally. She was running down a moonbeam that gleamed at my feet. Her hair flew out behind her in long chestnut curls and she was laughing as she ran, her light summer dress whipping round her in the wind. I started up. I was laughing too and the tears ran down my face. I caught her gently as she landed and I held her tightly to me.

I was still unconscious when the soldiers found me.

CHAPTER THIRTY

THE main door of the prisoner's cell swung open and four men walked slowly through. The prisoner turned from the window. The priest detached himself from the group and came towards him.

'It's time,' he said softly.

The prisoner nodded silently. Beads of sweat grew on his forehead.

They bound his hands behind his back and escorted him across to the cell to a small door on the other side which led to the death room. One warder stepped forward, unlocked the door and swung it open. The party moved forward but stopped again as the old warder started up.

'Excuse me,' he muttered as he squeezed his way through to the prisoner whom he seized by the hand.

'Innocent,' he said fervently. 'So help me you're innocent. If anybody hurt my missus that way I'd have done the same as you.'

Suddenly he felt embarrassed as all eyes were on him and he snatched his hand away.

'I just wanted him to know,' he said defiantly as he stepped back.

'Thank you,' the prisoner said softly and the death-room door swung closed.

CHAPTER THIRTY-ONE

THE old man stood by an empty grave below the charred farmhouse. On either side lay the graves of Sally and Katchemu.

He pulled out his pocket watch. 'He's dead,' he said to the farmers and the Africans who waited silently. 'Fill it in.'

The old man bowed his head in prayer as they began to shovel in the earth, and his mind echoed with the voices of his dead wife and children.

Several farmers lined up on either side of the grave.

'What are you doing?' the old man asked sharply.

'The peoples and me,' Van said sadly, 'we know that you can't get his body back from the prison to give him a proper burial. So me and the peoples, we're going to fire our rifles over the grave so loud that God in his Heaven is going to hear them and know that Terick's coming up.'

'What Van means,' one of the farmers cut in, 'is that we want to give Terick a military funeral. Is that all right with you?'

'That's good.' The old man smiled through his tears. 'Man, that's very good. Thank you. For me he died fighting in those rocks, not by some rope in a cell.' He turned to go. Peter and Dizarki helped him into his wheelchair.

'You'll stay and see that it's finished properly?' he asked, as the first volley rang out behind him.

Peter nodded silently.

He turned to Dizarki. 'You know that sign "Johannes' Dream" at the end of my lands?'

'Yes, my Mambo,' Dizarki said softly.

'We'll take it down, Dizarki,' the old man said sadly. 'It doesn't mean anything any more.'

THE END

MACAU

by Daniel Carney

MACAU: the most exciting city in the East – certainly the most lawless. a six-and-a-half mile haven for smugglers, spies and blockade runners. Home of a powerful criminal organisation – the Macau Syndicate – who have grown rich on the illicit gold trade.

DR SUN: whose favourite after-dinner trick at his own banquets was to shoot under the table at the legs of his guests, leaves a daughter. At twenty-five, Crystal Lily has inherited control of the Syndicate, but also his debts to the notorious 14K Triad based in Hong Kong, which must be paid in gold bullion before a fast-approaching deadline. Every day Crystal Lily fears the assassin's knife, for Thomas Wu – her father's personal secretary – had cast himself as Dr Sun's successor and hated the girl who robbed him of his inheritance.

NICOLAI: the Russian 'Snake Boat Man' had become a living legend as the foremost smuggler in the South China Seas. It is he Crystal Lily calls out of retirement to make one last crucial run for gold . . .

'A swashbuckling thriller written with infectious gusto'
WILBUR SMITH

'In the style of bestsellers like Tai-Pan and Shōgun . . . guaranteed to set its readers' pulses racing'
JOHN BARKHAM REVIEWS

0 552 12648 9   £2.50

UNDER A RAGING SKY

by Daniel Carney

To camp under a raging sky with a wild moon rising – that was Patrick Sillitoes's dream. An orphaned, raw young Englishman, in search of the untamed Africa of the cinema screen and *King Solomon's Mines*, he found himself trapped as a menial clerk in a huge company in Salisbury – his romantic dream abandoned for love of the beautiful, rich Judith.

But then he met a drunken, wild-eyed, raggedly-dressed old man who hypnotised him into longing for the touch of gold . . . and he followed the old man's lead through the wild veld, to the haunted pools of the Ruenya, the River of Gold.

Through hardship, exhaustion and sickness, their strange love-hate partnership held strong. Patrick became a hardened, lean, obsessive Gold-seeker, haunted always by a vision of Judith . . . scared that he had lost her forever . . .

0 552 11592 4   £2.50

OTHER FINE NOVELS AVAILABLE FROM CORGI BOOKS

WHILE EVERY EFFORT IS MADE TO KEEP PRICES LOW, IT IS SOMETIMES NECESSARY TO INCREASE PRICES AT SHORT NOTICE. CORGI BOOKS RESERVE THE RIGHT TO SHOW AND CHARGE NEW RETAIL PRICES ON COVERS WHICH MAY DIFFER FROM THOSE ADVERTISED IN THE TEXT OR ELSEWHERE.

THE PRICES SHOWN BELOW WERE CORRECT AT THE TIME OF GOING TO PRESS (SEPTEMBER '85).

☐	10808 1	**The Wild Geese**	Daniel Carney	£1.95
☐	11831 1	**Wild Geese II**	Daniel Carney	£1.75
☐	11592 4	**Under A Raging Sky**	Daniel Carney	£2.50
☐	12648 9	**Macau**	Daniel Carney	£2.50
☐	12464 8	**The Burning Mountain**	Alfred Coppel	£2.50
☐	12478 8	**The Dragon**	Alfred Coppel	£2.50
☐	12394 3	**34 East**	Alfred Coppel	£1.95
☐	11982 2	**The Hastings Conspiracy**	Alfred Coppel	£1.75
☐	12079 0	**The Apocalypse Brigade**	Alfred Coppel	£1.95
☐	12610 1	**On Wings Of Eagles**	Ken Follett	£2.50
☐	12180 5	**The Man From St. Petersburg**	Ken Follett	£2.50
☐	11810 9	**The Key to Rebecca**	Ken Follett	£1.95
☐	12417 6	**The Salamandra Glass**	A. W. Mykel	£2.50
☐	11850 8	**The Windchime Legacy**	A. W. Mykel	£2.50
☐	08713 0	**Poor No More**	Robert Ruark	£2.95
☐	07655 4	**The Honey Badger**	Robert Ruark	£2.95
☐	08392 5	**Something Of Value**	Robert Ruark	£2.95
☐	01440 0	**Uhuru**	Robert Ruark	£2.95
☐	12614 4	**The Haj**	Leon Uris	£2.95
☐	10565 1	**Trinity**	Leon Uris	£2.95
☐	08866 8	**QB VII**	Leon Uris	£2.50
☐	08384 4	**Exodus**	Leon Uris	£2.95
☐	08091 8	**Topaz**	Leon Uris	£2.95
☐	08385 2	**Mila 18**	Leon Uris	£2.95
☐	07300 8	**Armageddon**	Leon Uris	£2.95
☐	08521 9	**The Angry Hills**	Leon Uris	£1.95

All these books are available at your bookshop or newsagent, or can be ordered direct from the publisher. Just tick the titles you want and fill in the form below.

CORGI BOOKS, Cash Sales Department, P.O Box 11, Falmouth, Cornwall.

Please send cheque or postal order, no currency.

Please allow cost of book(s) plus the following for postage and packing:

U.K. CUSTOMERS – Allow 55p for the first book, 22p for the second book and 14p for each additional book ordered, to a maximum charge of £1.75.

B.F.P.O. & EIRE – Allow 55p for the first book, 22p for the second book plus 14p per copy for the next seven books, thereafter 8p per book.

OVERSEAS CUSTOMERS – Allow £1.00 for the first book and 25p per copy for each additional book.

NAME (Block letters) ....

ADDRESS ....

....